EARTHSONG

Also by Victor Kelleher

———————————— • ————————————

Forbidden Paths of Thual
The Hunting of Shadroth
Master of the Grove
Papio
The Green Piper
Taronga
The Makers
Baily's Bones
The Red King
Brother Night
Del-Del
To the Dark Tower
Where the Whales Sing
Parkland

EARTHSONG

Victor Kelleher

VIKING

Viking
Penguin Books Australia Ltd
487 Maroondah Highway, PO Box 257
Ringwood, Victoria 3134, Australia
Penguin Books Ltd
Harmondsworth, Middlesex, England
Viking Penguin, A Division of Penguin Books USA Inc.
375 Hudson Street, New York, New York 10014, USA
Penguin Books Canada Limited
10 Alcorn Avenue, Toronto, Ontario, Canada M4V 3B2
Penguin Books (N.Z.) Ltd
182–190 Wairau Road, Auckland 10, New Zealand

First published by Penguin Books Australia, 1995
10 9 8 7 6 5 4 3 2 1

Typeset in Plantin 12/13pt by Midland Typesetters, Maryborough, Victoria
Made and printed in Australia by Australian Print Group, Maryborough,
Victoria

National Library of Australia
Cataloguing-in-Publication data:

Kelleher, Victor, 1939–   .
Earthsong.
ISBN 0 670 86711 X.
I. Title.
A823.3

This project has been assisted by the Commonwealth Government through
the Australia Council, its arts funding and advisory body.

Part 1
SONG OF THE LAND

1

Anna sensed that something was wrong even before she glanced across at the nearest port and saw the dark of space beyond.

She sat up, feeling cold and stiff and slightly muzzy in the head. That at least was normal, what she would have expected after months of hiber-sleep. What wasn't normal was being woken like this, while the flight was still in progress. They had been told at the briefing that they would sleep right through until after they had landed. So what . . .?

A movement on the far side of the cabin attracted her attention. In the greenish glow of the revival lights she could see that Joe was also sitting up. With his face all puffy from sleep he looked far younger than his sixteen years, more like an outsized child than the capable person she knew him to be. Mind you, she thought ruefully, that was probably how she looked too.

Suddenly self-conscious, she ran both hands through her hair, and was surprised to find how long it had grown. As had her nails. But that was a good sign, wasn't it? Proof that they were near the end of their journey and not lost somewhere in between. Well, there was one sure way of finding out, and she was on the point of opening her mouth to speak when Joe got in ahead of her.

'What's going on?' he demanded, addressing the question not to her, but to the inner walls of the ship.

No answer. And Anna remembered then that to activate the identity of the ship they had to address it by name. Now what was it called? Something unlikely and curiously old-fashioned, to her ears anyway. Hurriedly she groped back through the details of the briefing, and with a rush it came to her.

'What's going on, Walter?' she queried, and the addition of that one word brought the interior of the cabin hummingly alive, the bright overhead lights flashing on.

'We are nearing our destination,' a voice answered – a careful, impersonal kind of voice which seemed to emanate from the surrounding walls, speaking to them with the measured calm of an older relative.

'But why wake us now?' Joe broke in impatiently.

There was a brief, apologetic pause. 'Because a fault has been detected.'

'A fault?' Anna and Joe looked at each other in momentary alarm.

Again that same hesitation, carrying with it a mute air of apology. 'I'm sorry to tell you that our heat shields have proved defective. Some have failed to activate.'

Heat shields? Was that all? Relieved, Anna swung both feet down from the capsule and stood up.

'Then send out that . . . what do you call it?'

'The Trog?' Walter asked helpfully.

4

'Yes, Trog, send him out to fix them.'

'I'm afraid that wouldn't help,' Walter replied, as polite as ever. 'You see, the ceramic shields are perfectly in order. It's the protective force field which refuses to activate.'

'D'you mean we're going to burn up?' Anna demanded, a hint of panic in her tone.

'Oh no, you need have no fear of that.' The voice's unruffled calm, as much as the words themselves, reassured her. 'The hull will overheat, that is all. According to my calculations the ceramic shields should prevent the ship from disintegrating. Within the cabin temperatures will rise, but not to fatal levels.'

'Then why wake us now?' Joe asked again. 'Why not keep to the original flight schedule?'

This time there was nothing apologetic about the slight delay in answering. If anything, it seemed to convey a suggestion of sadness.

'I am, as you are aware, an integrated system. That means my circuitry is distributed throughout the hull, and for that reason is vulnerable. I shall take steps to protect myself, of course, but still there may be some heat damage. It's impossible to say precisely what the effect will be. For example, I could suffer what in your terms would be a prolonged loss of consciousness. In such a state I would be incapable of carrying out my normal functions, which is why I have taken the precaution of waking you now. It is only a precaution, however. A more likely scenario is that I will merely undergo some form of personality change and will be different after the landing.'

'Different how?' Anna asked curiously.

'Again I cannot say. It will depend on the nature

5

of the damage. In the meantime I must warn you that entry into the planet's atmosphere will commence in a little over five minutes. I shall start counting down . . . now.'

On the far wall a digital clock immediately flashed on and began running backwards.

Five minutes! Anna exchanged a single excited glance with Joe, and together they made for the nearest port, their movements slow and stiff after months of inactivity.

The sight that greeted them there caused them both to suck in their breath. Outlined against the surrounding black was the home planet. Earth! Shimmering blue and interlaced with white, it looked exactly like the pictures they had been shown as children: photographs taken many centuries earlier, before Earth's climate had undergone changes so drastic that people had been driven off-world to Titan in order to survive.

'Home!' Anna breathed, amazed at her sense of attachment to this place she had never really known. A place which nobody had set foot on for many generations, because all those who stayed behind had perished. The small underwater sea-colonies had lasted longer than most, but eventually they too died out. Little by little their transmissions had failed, until one day not a single human voice reached across space between Earth and Titan.

'Three minutes to entry,' Walter droned in the background, interrupting the flow of her thoughts. 'Early indications are that the climate is fully restored. Oxygen levels have risen; carbon dioxide is within permissible limits; temperatures accord roughly with those of the twentieth century.'

'So it *has* healed itself!' Joe whispered excitedly,

not taking his eyes from the port. 'It's the same as it was before.'

'Not exactly the same,' she cautioned him. 'Remember there are no people left, no large land animals. Not as far as we can tell.'

He waved her objection aside. 'Yes, but the place itself, it's just like it used to be. It's done what we couldn't do – restored itself.'

'Maybe that's just as well for us,' Anna replied, and tried to laugh, but somehow those first moments of discovery were too serious for laughter.

Like Joe, she continued to contemplate the great cloud-streaked globe hanging there in the blackness of space. Their very own home planet! Healed at last. Its ruined climate, its fouled seas, all restored. The land waiting to be recolonised; ready for human history to begin again.

'Two minutes,' Walter warned them. 'The first parents would be advised to secure themselves within their capsules.'

The first parents! Anna relished the term as she lay down and strapped herself to the contoured mattress. Back on Titan, at the start of this project, she had been embarrassed by such a grandiose title. She and Joe, the first parents! It had sounded absurd. Almost as silly as calling them Adam and Eve. Yet here, now, it suddenly made sense. For already the transport and incubator ships, with their precious cargo of embryos, would have completed the journey from Titan. They were down there at that moment, great dark hulks nestled in some sub-tropical forest, waiting to be opened, to be inhabited, their banks of incubators ready to be stirred into life. She visualised the process that would follow: the way the frozen embryos, in their clear plastic wombs, would slowly begin to blossom, to bloom, to grow into healthy children who would one day move out from the home ships and repopulate the abandoned planet. Of course she and Joe would see only the beginning of the process. Altogether it would take generations, but still they would be remembered as the original parent figures. The very idea gave her a warm feeling.

'One minute to entry,' Walter intoned, breaking in upon her thoughts once again. Then, more chillingly: 'Calculations to hand indicate that we cannot rendezvous with the transport ships. Without full shield protection, the projected angle of descent is too steep. We would burn up. I am arranging now to enter at a lesser angle. Impossible as yet to calculate our exact landing site, which will depend on ongoing adjustments. At a rough estimate we will probably overshoot the rendezvous point by more than a thousand kilometres.'

'Did he say a *thousand*?' That was Joe, far more alarmist than Anna, his face turned in anguish towards her. 'How the hell will we get back to the transports?'

The digital clock was showing only twenty seconds.

'What are your plans after landing, Walter?' she demanded urgently.

'Too early to say,' he replied in a clipped, economical tone. 'First duty to land you safely. After, circumstances permitting, to fly you back.'

Only ten seconds left!

'And if you're damaged?' she nearly shouted. 'If your personality is changed, like you said? What then?'

'Hopefully still function,' he began cryptically. 'In event of personality breakdown . . .'

8

The rest was blotted out by the rush and roar of entry. Clutching onto the shaking sides of her capsule, she glanced towards Joe who was riding out the storm with gritted teeth, his eyes firmly closed. She was about to follow his example when she caught sight of the far port. It no longer showed the blackness of space, nor even the shimmering blue of the planet, but rather a great arc of light which grew brighter with each passing second.

She knew, with a lurching sense of fear, what that brilliant light meant. The ceramic shields were burning up, peeling away in a searing tail of flame. Already she could feel the temperature in the cabin rising, the air becoming stiflingly hot. She tried to breathe and felt she was drawing the outside flames inside her, their hungry tips probing to the innermost reaches of her lungs. And her throat! So dry that she licked thirstily at the sweat pouring down her face, her lips numb with terror. More sweat ran from her limbs, soaking her. And still the noise and buffeting increased, the circle of the port now blinding, like a new-born sun.

'Walter!' she cried out in anguish – or tried to, but only a feeble whisper emerged, and that was lost in the surrounding din.

What was the use of appealing to him anyway? What could he do in all this ... this ...? As she groped for a way of describing her mounting despair, a single word came to mind, forced upon her by the gathering flame at the window. Hell. Yes, that was what they were plummeting into. Hell! A burning place in which she was forever doomed ... doomed to ...

Mercifully she never had to complete that thought. She, the cabin, the light at the port, were all eclipsed by a darkness deeper and wider than space itself. Or so it felt as it rolled over her and, wavelike, drew her down into the less turbulent depths of unconsciousness.

*   *   *

It was the silence which helped bring her round. That and the sudden clink of metal on metal.

Her first thought was that she had been roused from hiber-sleep. But then why were her lips so dry and salty? And why did her clothes feel so uncomfortable, as though stiff with dried sweat? Anyone would think she had been through some kind of fiery ordeal.

Ordeal?

Everything came back to her then, and she snapped her eyes open in relief just as that telltale clink of metal sounded again.

It was Trog, the onboard transformer, lumbering across the cabin towards her. His more imaginative half, Og, had begun unfolding from his chest cavity, as if ready for immediate use.

'Who activated you?' she croaked as he rumbled past.

'No external agent necessary,' Trog chirped back in his usual official manner. 'Automatic activation whenever craft suffers damage.'

So, it wasn't Walter who had released the robot, as she had hoped. Was he even intact after their entry? She gazed quickly around the interior of the cabin. That at least seemed unchanged, no trace of burning anywhere. On the other hand, what about the outer hull? If that was badly burned . . .!

'How much damage is there?' she asked, hoping Walter would respond.

But to her dismay there was no sound from the surrounding walls, and it was Trog, practical as ever, who eventually answered.

'Damage is extensive. Request permission to transform.'

And Og, drawing on his range of popular quotations and old sayings: 'Two pairs of hands are better than one.'

She ignored the request, too miserable to care what they did. Without Walter there seemed little to be gained by carrying out repairs. Hadn't he said they would end up a thousand or more kilometres off target? What hope did they have of getting to the transports unaided? This ship *was* Walter; Walter *was* this ship – they were one and the same. If he had been wiped out during entry, then she and Joe were stranded in an empty shell.

Shakily she unclipped her safety harness and sat up. Joe was just coming round, his eyelids fluttering as he moaned softly to himself. She went over to release him, and he surfaced with a start, his eyes instantly focussed, revealing none of the confusion she had felt on waking.

'Did he survive?' he demanded, and lurched so suddenly to his feet that he had to steady himself against the bulkhead.

'I . . . I don't think so,' she stammered, and to her shame felt close to tears.

Either Joe didn't notice or he was trying to spare her feelings because he turned away and tipped his face to the ceiling.

'Can you hear me?' he called. 'Are you still with us?'

They waited, the silence stretching on hopelessly.

'He must have burned up,' Anna sighed, trying to

keep the anxiety from her voice.

Clearly Joe wasn't prepared to accept that. Not yet. Glancing round, he noticed Trog standing by, his blunt face raised expectantly.

'Separate and get outside,' he said, pointing to the airlock. 'Both of you. Look for holes in the hull; inspect the inner lining for damage. Report back what you find.'

Straight away Og folded out from Trog's chest cavity. 'Many hands make light work,' he observed in a squeaky voice as he set off after his companion.

Before they could reach the airlock, however, Anna called them back. 'Wait a minute. You know the procedures as well as I do. No one's supposed to use that airlock without first checking external conditions.'

'What's there to check?' Joe said with a shrug. 'This is Earth, isn't it?'

The two robots, meanwhile, had stopped halfway to the door.

'Conflicting orders,' Trog remarked. 'Please clarify.'

'Too many cooks spoil the broth,' Og complained.

'Anyway,' Joe added, ignoring the robots for the moment, 'we can't monitor external conditions from in here. We have no access to the ship's instruments.'

'But we could have landed in the sea, in the tree-tops, *anywhere*,' Anna pointed out, and led the way to the nearest port.

They were confronted by neither trees nor water, but by a bleak upland landscape in which nothing lived, nothing grew. In the fading afternoon light, all they could see was snow: wind-borne flecks of it whirling past the port; the ground all but covered by a thick white blanket, with just the occasional spike of black rock poking through. Icicles, some a metre or two in length, hung from the rocks, their crystal shafts visibly vibrating from the force of the wind.

'My God!' Joe exclaimed. 'It looks freezing out there!'

Anna couldn't help but agree, and instinctively she hugged herself, as though warding off the cold. Except that there in the cabin, as she realised instantly, it wasn't cold at all. Even in her light tunic she felt perfectly comfortable. Her suspicions aroused, she searched for other signs. The strip lights, for instance, they were still on. And the air, there was nothing stagnant about it. If she listened hard, she could just detect the whisper of the air-conditioning unit.

'What's the matter?' Joe asked, worried by her silence.

She grabbed him by the wrist, her face curiously intent. 'The onboard systems – the lights, the air, everything – they're all working! If the ship was dead they'd have shut down.'

He nodded, only half convinced. 'But if we can't get any response . . .' he began, and she cut straight across him.

'Hold on a minute!' She was thinking aloud now. 'Let's go back to what it was like during entry. It got so hot that we blacked out, right? Which was our brains' way of closing us down. Of protecting us. Of getting us through a really testing time.'

'I still don't see . . .' he began again, and stopped as a smile creased her cheeks.

'The ship's a kind of brain, isn't it? And it was trying to survive, the same as us. So why should it have acted any different?'

'Are you saying it blacked out?'

'In a way. When the heat was at its worst, it would

have closed off everything but basic support systems. Including its conscious mind, the way it did on the long voyage here. If you like, it went into a kind of coma. Well, there's only one way of bringing it out.'

She saw understanding dawn slowly on his face.

'You mean call it by name? Reactivate it all over again?'

There was no need for her to answer, both of them switching their gaze to the walls.

'Walter?' she whispered. 'Can you hear me?'

She was waiting for a calm, impersonal voice, not for the ripple of mischievous laughter that spread softly through the cabin.

Laughter? But no ship was programmed for that! Not even Og was capable of humour.

'What the hell's going on?' Joe demanded, searching about him.

Again laughter swelled through the narrow space – childlike, almost capricious, as if a child were hidden somewhere in the walls.

'Walter!' Anna repeated more urgently. 'Is that really you?'

The laughter died away and was followed by an unknown voice. High-pitched, immature, it might have belonged to an eight-year-old.

'All right, I give up,' it said with a playful chuckle. 'You've found me. Now it's your turn to hide.'

2

'Hide?' Anna exclaimed. 'What on earth are you talking about?'

'On Earth?' the young piping voice took her up, and burst into the same mischievous laughter as before. 'Oh yes, I like that. You sure get used to the local conditions quickly.'

'Listen to me,' she interrupted, feeling oddly schoolmarmish, as though lecturing an unruly pupil. 'You are Walter, aren't you?'

The voice hiccupped and gave a long-suffering sigh. 'You can call me Walt if you like.'

'All right, Walter,' she responded, ignoring the invitation. 'This is no time for games, as you should know better than anyone.'

'No time for games!' he echoed her. 'What else is there to do around here? Have you looked outside? At what it's like?' And he burst into song, his voice trilling childishly on the high notes:

The north wind doth blow
And we shall have snow.
What shall poor Walter do then, poor thing?

'This is no time for silly nursery rhymes either,' Anna came back at him.

15

'Oh, you want something more grown up. Is that it? How about this?'

Blow, blow, thou winter wind,
Thou art not so unkind as man's . . .

Joe, who until then had been looking on in astonishment, suddenly slapped his hand against the nearest bulkhead. 'That's enough!' he shouted. 'Here we are God knows how far from the transports, and all you can do is spout poetry. Og is *supposed* to talk like that, but you . . .!'

'One thousand four hundred and seventy-eight kilometres from the transports to be exact,' Walter informed him. 'That's as the crow flies, of course. Though how anyone would get a crow to travel that far is beyond me.'

'I'm not interested in crows!' Joe yelled, more frustrated than ever. '*We're* the ones who have to fly back to the rendezvous point, and it's your job to see we get there.'

'No can do, O Mighty One,' Walter replied.

Joe's face had gone bright red, but before he could begin yelling again Anna placed a hand on his shoulder.

'Are you disobeying a direct order, Walter?' she asked quietly.

It was Trog who answered her. 'No direct order yet given,' he announced to the company in general.

'The Trog's right,' Walter said with a laugh. 'Clever little fella, isn't he? Even if he *is* a bit dull. Personally I find Og's programming a lot more fun.'

'You know what I mean,' Anna insisted. 'Are you refusing to fly us back or not?'

'Not refusing,' he said brightly. 'Just telling you I

16

can't. And you know what'll happen if you order me to do the impossible. I'll probably blow what circuits I have left.' To show what he meant, he began to make fizzing, crackling noises as if he really were breaking down.

'You'll have to explain this to us, Walter,' Anna went on, curbing her impatience. 'Why is it so impossible to fly us to the transports?'

'Because I don't have a magic carpet. You know, like in the stories, where Aladdin or Sinbad or someone calls to his genie. That's me,' he added, a note of enthusiasm creeping into his voice. '"Genie," he says, "fly me to ... to ... wherever." And *wop*! There's this carpet with the front edge all curled up like a toboggan. And *whoosh*! Before you can say abracadabra they're up in the clouds and zooming along so fast that the G-force alone would blow them to kingdom come.'

'What's he going on about now?' Joe complained helplessly.

'Keep to the point, Walter,' Anna warned him.

'The point? Okay. The engines were heat-strained during entry. They're finished, kaput, messed up, broken down, mashed, smashed, boiled, fried, baked, wrecked, ruined, written off, crunched, despoiled, done for, wasted, *whammoed* ...' He paused as if for breath and collapsed into wheezy laughter. 'Or just about, anyway. At full strength they could barely get us off the ground. Or in this case the snow. Talking of snow, have you seen those icicles? Longer than Sinbad's sword. No, wait a minute, he would have used one of those scimitar things. All right, longer than Merlin's wand. How about that for ...?'

'Shut up!' Joe roared at the empty spaces of the cabin. And in the sudden hush: 'Just keep your mind

17

on the engines, understand? Now, why can't they be fixed? You can work out what's wrong, and we have Trog and Og on board to carry out the repairs.'

Walter let out another of his long-suffering sighs. 'Stripping down warp-capacity engines isn't exactly child's play.' He gave the briefest of snickers. 'Except for this child, naturally. It's a delicate business requiring specialist tools which we don't have. Even if we had the tools, it would still be way beyond those two ham-fisted pozzos.'

'Inaccurate description of transformers,' Trog commented.

While Og chimed in with: 'Sticks and stones may break our bones, but names can never hurt us.'

'What about contacting Titan then?' Joe went on, undeterred. 'They may be able to help.'

'Can't be done,' Walter responded. 'The transmitters were burned away. Gone, no more, all over with, dead, defunct, dissolved, disappeared, annihilated, gone phut, fizzled out, perished, expired, vanished, vapourised . . .'

Anna waited for him to grind to a halt before asking bleakly: 'So are you saying we're stuck here?'

He gave a simulated version of an embarrassed cough. 'Well . . . not for ever maybe . . . but at least for a while.'

She and Joe exchanged glances. Was Walter trying to ease the blow or simply being evasive?

'How long exactly?' she pressed him.

'Long enough to play a few games,' he said in a perfect imitation of her earlier schoolmarmish voice. 'Like hide-and-seek for instance. Or better still, I-spy. Ah yes, that's the game for a snowy day. So, who's to start? Me again? Right, I spy with my little eye something beginning with . . . H and O.'

'Horrible Og,' Og answered promptly.

'Not fair!' Walter screeched. 'He tuned in. That means I have another turn. Everyone ready? Here's a really hard one. I spy with my little . . .'

Anna didn't bother to listen. She was already signalling to Joe, and at his nod of agreement she said loudly: 'Time to close down, Walter.'

'Do I have to?' He sounded now like a sulky little boy being asked to go to bed.

To bed? The idea alone made Anna glance towards the port which was beginning to darken.

'Everyone goes to sleep when it gets dark,' she said reasonably.

'Not me. I never need sleep.'

She had a sudden inspiration. 'Then just pretend.'

'Like in a game?' he asked enthusiastically.

'Yes, like in a game.'

He gave an extravagant yawn. 'Are there any bedtime stories in this game?'

'Sometimes there are, but not tonight. The parents are tired too.'

'Later maybe?'

'Yes, later,' she promised. 'Now sleep, Walter, sleep.'

The atmosphere in the cabin seemed to change slightly, and she knew he was gone.

'Good riddance to bad rubbish,' Og observed.

'You two can close down as well,' she informed the transformers, and without complaint they packed themselves together and slotted into their wall cavity.

Alone at last, she and Joe looked at each other.

'What do you make of that?' she asked.

Joe ran one hand through his hair. 'He's reverted, that's pretty clear. It's like he's gone back to being a child. But how the hell did it happen? I didn't even

19

know he had that capacity. I thought if he was damaged, he'd just lose some of his functions.'

'Maybe the engineers on Titan made him differently,' Anna said. 'They could have programmed him in stages. You know, like growing up. That way he'd have a more human personality.'

'Yeah, that would explain it. The heat must have destroyed all the later development. It left him as a kid again.'

'A clever kid, though,' Anna pointed out. 'Did you notice how quick he was? And how he brought the conversation back to where it started? Games, they're all he's really interested in.'

'Don't forget stories.'

'Oh yes, those too.'

'So what do we do about him?'

Anna shrugged. 'I don't know. Without him we're stuck. We'd never get back to the transports.'

'We could try walking,' Joe suggested.

'What, for nearly fifteen hundred kilometres? Through all that ice and snow? We're not equipped for those conditions.'

'It may not be like that all the way.'

'No, we could run into mountains, seas, anything. What would we do then?'

Joe stared moodily at the dark circle of the port. 'Haven't a clue. Right now I'm starving. Let's get something to eat and then think again.'

'We need Walter to access the food stores,' she reminded him.

'Not if we use the emergency rations.' And stooping beneath his capsule he opened a small compartment and took out two containers of food and drink.

For a while they ate in silence – Joe with a puzzled, slightly trapped expression on his face, as though he couldn't work out which way to turn. Anna, by contrast, looked merely thoughtful, her forehead furrowed with concentration.

'I've been thinking,' she said as soon as they finished their meal. 'If you want a child to do a difficult job, the best way is to turn the whole thing into a game, or to make it part of a story. Then they're so busy playing that it never occurs to them to regard it as work. It stays fun no matter how hard it gets.'

Joe nodded. 'Yeah, and Walter's fascinated by games *and* stories. The problem is, how does that help us? The ship still won't fly.'

'That's true, but Walter's clever. If we can involve him in the right kind of game, he may come up with ways of getting us out of here.'

'You reckon you could fool him into doing that?'

'It's worth a try.'

So saying, she switched her attention to the surrounding cabin. 'Walter,' she whispered gently. 'Time to wake up.'

She was greeted by a loud yawn. 'What?' he exclaimed in a sleepy voice. 'Is bedtime over already? But it's still dark.'

'I know. I just woke you to tell you that story I promised.'

There was a gurgle of appreciative laughter. 'A story! Wow, this is more like it. Hold on while I get myself sitting comfortably. Aah, that's better. Away you go.'

She took a deep breath. 'Well, this story's about . . .'

'Hey! That's not how stories start,' Walter objected. 'You've got to do it right.'

'Once upon a time,' she began again, and was rewarded with a sigh of contentment, 'there was this

21

spaceship stranded on the surface of a planet called Earth. It was no ordinary ship, but as alive as the people on board. What's more, it knew it had landed in the wrong place. Somehow it had to make its way back to . . .'

'Hey!' Walter broke in for the second time. 'I already know this story.'

'Only how it begins. Not how it goes on.'

'So how does it go on?'

This was the difficult part, and she paused to gather her thoughts. 'I can't just *tell* you that, Walter, because this isn't that kind of story. This is the sort of story that has to be acted out by people. Joe and I and the transformers, and you especially, we all have a role to play. We have to make the story happen.'

'You mean like in a game?'

It was what she had been hoping he would say. 'Yes, a game that won't stop, not even for a minute, until we reach the transports.'

'Wow! That's what I call a game,' he began with relish, and stopped short. 'But hang on. How can we act it out? I've already told you, the engines are just about ruined. They couldn't fly us anywhere.'

'Then we won't fly,' Joe added quickly. 'We'll find another way of travelling. Can you think of anything?'

The overhead lights flickered slightly, and then, in the slyest tone Walter had used so far: 'Can I do what I want with the ship? Like . . . like turn it into something else?'

'Anything, just as long as it works.'

The voice sounded slyer than ever now. 'So I'll be the boss of the whole ship?'

'Most of the time,' Anna agreed guardedly. 'Think

22

of yourself as the captain, and the rest of us as the crew.'

The laughter was back, a gurgle of pure delight. 'Captain Walter!' he crowed. 'The scourge of the seven seas. I'll be Captain Hook and Long John Silver and Blackbeard all rolled into one. Avast there, ye lubbers! When they see my Jolly Roger flying from the mainmast they'll wish they'd never been born.'

'We're wasting time, Walter,' Anna reminded him gently. 'That's an old game. Let's play the new one.'

'Ah yes, the new one.' He made the noise of someone clearing his throat. 'Are you ready?'

'If you are.'

'Well, ready or not, here we go. Action stations! All hands on deck! And I mean *all*!'

There was a click as Trog stepped from his place in the wall; and a second click as Og unfolded from Trog's chest cavity.

'Awaiting further orders,' Trog bleeped.

'No rest for the wicked,' Og echoed him.

'Able seaman Anna,' Walter continued, 'you'll conduct the work party out through the airlock and . . .'

All at once his voice faltered, only to be replaced by a faint rustling. Or was this new sound perhaps coming from elsewhere? Anna, listening intently, found it hard to be sure.

'What is it?' she and Joe asked together.

'Hush!' Walter cautioned them.

The rustling continued, overlaid at last by a furtive whisper from Walter, his voice lower and far less childlike than before.

'Red alert!' he breathed. 'We're boarded! I repeat: red alert, we're boarded!'

Joe half suppressed an impatient sigh. 'You heard

23

Anna a minute or two back,' he said wearily. 'We're not interested in old games about pirates and stuff. It's the new game that matters now.'

Walter's answer was softer still, as though meant for no other ears but theirs.

'This *is* the new game. Like I said, red alert! We're boarded!'

3
———— • ————

As the outer door of the airlock slid aside, Anna tightened her grip on the steel bar and stepped through, her heavy boots crunching on the drifted snow. The wind had dropped, the air now so brittle-cold that it made her cheeks tingle.

'Keep your eyes open,' Walter whispered through the tiny speaker in her ear, and she shook her head irritably. What else did he expect her to do?

Warily she gazed about her. Despite the absence of the moon, the night was not particularly dark. The snow-covered landscape seemed to give off a pale, slightly luminous glow; and overhead the great sweep of the Milky Way was clotted with stars, glittering clusters of them that tipped the nearby rocks with silver and coaxed blue-white beams of light from the crystal depths of the icicles.

'Check the ground for tracks,' Walter hissed, and she fumbled for her headlamp and switched it on.

In its circular beam she saw them: small scurrying marks in the snow, like twin sets of tiny footprints. Another mark creased the snow between the footprints, this one harder to identify because it was little more than a thin unbroken line, as though whatever had made the tracks had been dragging something behind.

Now what . . .? she wondered, but was suddenly distracted. There was a beep of warning from Trog, who had left the airlock with her, and she looked up just as the creature itself crept from a crevice in the rocks.

Her first instinct was to defend herself, jerking the steel bar up before her face. Then, with a sigh of relief, she recognised the thing for what it was. A rat.

Admittedly it was bigger than any she had ever seen, with shaggy fur and a thick cord of tail, but it was a rat just the same. And she was about to let the steel bar drop to her side when, instead of scurrying off, the animal turned directly towards her. There was no mistaking its aggression, the gleam of its eyes catching the starlight. Another second and it might have leaped for her throat, but again Trog beeped, and this time, as a purely reflex action, she flung the bar.

The rat avoided it with ease, the bar lodging harmlessly in the snow. Next, it did something that was both curious and also oddly disturbing. With a slow twist of the head, it looked deliberately from her to the bar and back again, as if establishing the link between the two.

Or was the rat doing more than that? she asked herself with a sudden shiver. Was it perhaps establishing that she was now unarmed, someone who could be attacked with ease? That was certainly how it seemed, and yet surely no rat could think so clearly.

The animal itself put her doubts to rest by letting out a high squeak and then rushing forward with renewed purpose, its teeth gleaming.

It had reckoned without Trog, however. Stepping into its path just as it leaped clear of the snow, he caught it effortlessly in one clamp-like hand. There was a whirring noise, and before Anna could protest, his hydraulic grip tightened on the squirming animal which instantly went slack.

'Total systems failure,' Trog announced, and tossed the dead creature well clear of the ship, its body falling with a thud onto the snow.

It was then that Anna became aware of Walter's voice whispering insistently in her ear.

'. . . not the only one. There are more rats in the fuselage. You may need help. Stay where you are and I'll send Joe out.'

'No.' She breathed the word into the wire-thin mouthpiece. 'We agreed someone should stay on board. I can see to it.'

'Well, be quick.' He gave an impish chuckle. 'Whatever they're doing, they . . . they . . . tickle!'

Although she could not have said why, she found his laughter distracting. Something about the present situation warned her that it was more serious than Walter suspected. Whatever the reason, she tugged the speaker from her ear and let it hang loosely against her neck. Then, with Walter's voice reduced to a background murmur, she retrieved her weapon and led the way around the ship, her booted feet squeaking on the compacted snow.

As she had suspected, the ship's ceramic shields were badly damaged. Blackened and twisted, they jutted out from the forward section of the hull like crippled hands. In places they had been burned paper-thin, their surfaces pitted and cracked; and it was behind one of the worst of these cracks that she located the hole in the hull.

It was not much more than a hand's breadth wide, and crouched within it was a rat. Even as she watched, the animal tore out a length of blackened wire with its teeth and dropped it to the snow. There

27

a second rat retrieved it and dashed off into the dark, its place immediately taken by another animal, with head already raised expectantly to the hole.

Anna wouldn't have believed it possible if she hadn't seen it with her own eyes. Rats acting like ... like robots or humans! Or was she being unreasonable? She knew from experience that many animals were by no means stupid. Why then shouldn't they organise themselves like this? Surely it was a natural development here in this harsh climate where survival was a constant struggle.

Or so she tried to convince herself, too taken aback to do more than stand there looking on.

Not so Trog. Responding to instructions from Walter, he reached up, plucked the rat from the hole, and sent it spinning off into the night. The rat waiting on the snow met the same fate, squealing in protest as it was flung aside. Other animals, their eyes tinged a pinkish red, watched from the shadows, none daring to advance. Especially when Trog pulled a sheet of metal from a slot in his body, rotated his free hand until he had exposed the point of an arc welder, and rapidly welded the hole closed.

'All systems protected,' he intoned, and trudged back to the airlock.

Still slightly bewildered, Anna followed more slowly. That was why she spotted the bloody ritual being enacted some twenty or thirty metres from the ship, out on the shadowy surface of the snow.

The dead rat which Trog had discarded earlier was now encircled by rats. As far as Anna could tell they were standing guard, protecting the carcass while one of their number rapidly dismembered it. Horrified, she watched as first the hind legs were chewed off, then each of the forelimbs, and after that the head and tail. When it could be reduced no further, companion rats snatched up the separate portions; and in a tight protective wedge, flanked by the biggest amongst them, the whole group moved off into the night.

Nothing was left on the snow but a bloody smudge, and for some minutes Anna couldn't take her eyes off it. What *was* going on? If she had not known otherwise, she would have sworn that the scene she had just witnessed was the work of some higher intelligence. Of someone like Walter, for instance, secretly directing the rats from a safe vantage point. Except that was impossible. No such robotic minds had existed when people had fled the ailing planet; and even if they had been developed by the undersea colonies, they couldn't have survived the extinction of the colonies themselves. Abandoned on a people-less planet, they would have mouldered away during the centuries that followed.

Mystified, her eyes riveted to that bloody stain on the snow, she was unaware of the furtive movements all about her. Of lithe, noiseless shadows creeping across the snow to her left and right. But for Walter's voice, screeching tinnily from the speaker hanging against her neck, she might not have noticed them at all. Or not until it was too late.

'Watch . . .! . . . in here! . . . as fast as . . .!' she could hear him shouting – mere fragments of instruction that made little sense.

What did he want now? she wondered vaguely, still stunned by the memory of that awful dismemberment, and she fumbled the speaker back into her ear.

'Yes . . .?'

His voice boomed inside her head, startlingly loud. 'Get out of there! While you still can!'

His tone was enough to alert her, and straight away she saw them: small groups of rats creeping towards her on every side. The nearest of them had already gathered into a spear-shaped formation, and as she turned to face them they charged.

A single sweep of the steel bar dispatched the lead rats, sending them skidding across the snow; but the rest came on relentlessly, scrambling over the bodies of their fallen companions. She backed away, swinging the bar a second time, felling more of them. From the corner of her eye she glimpsed another group closing in at a run, and she whirled around, hitting out as hard as she could, the impact of steel on flesh jarring her wrist. Yet she couldn't keep them all at bay. She realised that even as a sinuous shape ran up her leg and small grasping feet clutched at the loose cloth of her jacket. With a horrified cry she used her free hand to knock it aside, and felt more of those grasping feet drag down on the bar itself. She tried to pull it free, but it was firmly lodged in a tight mass of bodies, and before she could let go one of the rats extricated itself from the rest and scurried up her arm.

It was her worst fear. A part of her mind wanted to give in completely, paralysed by the horror of what was happening; but a more detached part of herself forced her to fight on. Shuddering with distaste, she plucked the thing from her shoulder and held it squirming in both hands. Just for a second, perhaps less, the rat's face and hers were barely half an arm's length apart, and in that brief time she saw . . . What? A glint of something in those furious eyes: something she couldn't quite identify, but which she knew did not belong there.

Whatever it was, it unnerved her so completely

that she slackened her grip enough for the rat to break free. It landed on her face with a sickening plop and held on fiercely, its thick fur blocking her nose and mouth, its sharp muzzle prying for her eyes. And the musty stench of it! The snuffling insistence of that searching mouth! And those scrabbling feet!

It was all too much, rendering her powerless. This is the end, she thought, recalling with a shudder how the other group of rats had dealt with their dead companion, leaving behind only a bloody stain on the snow. Was that to be her fate too? She knew it was, for more of the animals were already swarming up her legs. As she slumped to her knees, borne down by their weight, she begged silently for it to be over soon, steeling herself for what was to come.

Only to feel the soft fleshy body being jerked free of her face. She didn't dare open her eyes, not yet, but oh the joy of breathing the clean frosty air. She sucked it greedily into her lungs as the rest of her attackers were torn away and hurled squealing into the darkness.

She looked then and saw Trog standing solidly beside her, wielding his hands like weapons.

'Safety margin narrowing,' he intoned, clubbing aside a particularly large rat and fending off another. 'Return to ship without delay.'

She needed no further encouragement, and with Trog bringing up the rear she made a dash for safety, urged on by Walter's shrill cries.

Joe met her inside the airlock and she fell into his arms, sobbing with relief.

'Thank God!' he burst out, helping her through to the cabin. 'I thought they were going to eat you alive!'

'Still living tissue not suitable for food,' Trog corrected him.

Og, meanwhile, sealed the inner door with the comment: 'One person's meat is another's poison.'

Of them all, Walter was the only one who remained silent, waiting for Anna to collect herself; and when he finally did speak, he sounded different – not just calmer, but also more thoughtful.

'I can see I'll have to revise my memory banks,' he observed soberly. 'I was taught on Titan that small life-forms like rats are fairly harmless. Now we know they're not. They must have evolved while human beings were away. They seem to have developed greater powers of organisation.'

Anna dashed the last tears from her eyes. 'It's more than just organisation,' she said quietly.

'Really?' Some of the curious little boy crept back into his tone. 'What is it, then?'

'It's . . . it's . . .' She visualised again that unsettling glint in the rat's eyes as it had struggled between her hands. It had been so familiar, that look – a bit like gazing into a distorting mirror and seeing someone both alien and recognisable – and yet try as she might she could not say exactly what those eyes had told her.

'Go on,' Joe whispered, squeezing her hand.

'I don't know,' she added lamely. 'They were too smart for rats, that's all, even rats that have evolved. When they were closing in, I had this creepy feeling that somebody else was directing them.'

'Somebody else!' Walter repeated, a bubble of childish laughter breaking through. 'You mean some superbrain with a mouth who wants to eat people?' He let out a long rumbling burp. 'Aah, a female of the species, my favourite little snack.'

32

'Shut up, Walter!' Joe reprimanded him. 'Can't you see she's still upset?'

'. . . er . . . yes . . . um . . . sorry.' He gave one of his embarrassed coughs. 'It's just that apart from us and the transports, there're no higher forms of intelligence anywhere on this planet.'

'Your memory banks may be wrong again,' Joe pointed out.

'My scanners aren't though, and they detect nothing much bigger than a rat in this whole area.'

'Never mind what your scanners say,' Anna insisted. 'I'm telling you something funny's going on out there. I felt it.'

'What you *felt*,' Walter argued enthusiastically, 'was fear. You came face to face with real danger, like in all the best stories. And there was I thinking that to reach the transports all we had to do was follow a kind of obstacle course. Pretty dull compared with this, eh? People-eating rats! And that's only the beginning. Who knows what we'll encounter at the bottom of this mountain? I can hardly wait to find out.'

Good as his word, he issued a voiceless command, and both transformers turned abruptly and would have made for the airlock if Joe hadn't called them back.

'No one else is going out there tonight,' he said decisively. 'It's too dangerous.'

'But . . .'

'Joe's right,' Anna added. 'If we lose the transformers we're in real trouble. Better wait until morning when we can see what's going on.'

'Are you serious?' Walter jeered. 'What, give in to a bunch of *rodents*? Puny old rats! Where's your courage? Where's your pride? Where's . . .?'

'Where's your *sense*?' Joe interrupted impatiently. 'Imagine what would have happened to Anna if Trog had reached her a few seconds later. She'd have had no eyes. How do you feel about that?'

There was a telling silence.

'Well, the same thing could happen to Trog,' Joe went on, ramming the point home. 'His eyes are the most sensitive part of him. You know that.'

A breathy sigh issued from the walls. 'Yes, I suppose you're right. The morning will be better. Just as long as I don't have to go back to sleep. It's so boring when you close me down. Is it okay if I stand guard for the rest of the night? I won't make a sound, I promise.'

'All right, if you really want to.'

His sigh this time was one of pure contentment. 'Goodnight,' he whispered, 'sleep tight, and ... and ...'

'Yes?'

He delayed answering for a few moments as if embarrassed by what he wanted to say. 'A special goodnight to ... to you, Anna,' he stammered out. 'I ... I'm glad the rats didn't get you.'

He said nothing more after that, and minutes later the lights in the cabin had been dimmed, the transformers had folded themselves back into their wall cavity, and Joe and Anna were ready for bed. After their months of hiber-sleep, the tensions of the last few hours had left them both feeling exhausted. But on the point of climbing into her capsule, Anna hesitated, haunted still by the rat's glinting eyes and by the remembered plop of its body on her upturned face. In those few seconds of terror she had felt horribly alone, abandoned by everyone. And now, faced with the long night ahead, that same feeling of isolation swept over her again. What if she dreamed about the rat? What if it pursued her through the empty realms of sleep? Here, alone in her own capsule, there was no one she could turn to – no one but the clutching dark. It would be the same as out there on the snow before Trog arrived. The memory made her shiver despite the warmth of the cabin. No, she couldn't bear that to happen again, and on impulse she stole across to Joe's capsule and climbed in beside him.

It had been decided back on Titan that for practical reasons they would not share a bed until after the installation here on Earth was firmly established. Yet no one had foreseen how everything would go wrong ... how they'd miss their rendezvous and be marooned a long way from the transports, on a planet that contained untold dangers. All of that changed the rules, didn't it? At least for this one night.

Joe seemed to agree because he welcomed her without question. Lying there together in the dark, they waited for Walter to express his disapproval. He *was* the guardian of the project after all. But minutes passed and, true to his promise, he kept to his lonely vigil, the stillness of the cabin undisturbed.

'You know,' Anna whispered as they prepared for sleep, 'I think maybe Walter's started to grow up already.'

4

———————•———————

'All hands on deck!' Walter shrilled, sending the transformers tumbling from their cavity.

Anna woke more slowly, feeling wonderfully rested and secure, her encounter with the rats like a distant memory.

Joe stirred beside her. 'What, morning already?' he groaned, and she left him to wake fully while she padded across to the nearest port.

Outside there was no sign of the rats. More snow had fallen overnight, so even the bloodstain had disappeared. Now early morning sunlight slanted down onto a deserted landscape, the long banks of unsullied snow so dazzlingly white that she had to shield her eyes.

'Where d'you reckon the rats have gone to?' Joe asked, shuffling up beside her.

'I have no idea. Maybe they're nocturnal.'

'I didn't think they were,' he began, and was interrupted by Walter.

'A likely craft hovering off the port bow,' he declared in his best pirate voice. 'Look lively, my hearties. Scramble aloft and check its ensign.'

'Oh come on, Walter,' Anna protested, thinking he was joking. 'Give us a chance to wake up before you start your fun and games.'

'What's wrong with fun and games?' he answered petulantly. 'Or is *this* how you expect me to talk?' He switched to formal computer mode: 'Sensors detect airborne life-form in vicinity of ship. Intentions unknown. Advise monitoring of all movements.'

Airborne? Anna picked out that one word just as a shadow flitted across the snow beside the ship. Hastily she pressed her face to the port and squinted aloft, up into the clear blue of the sky. Nothing appeared for some moments, then the shadow was back, and high above it the winged shape of a large white bird. It was riding the wind, its wings barely moving, its head swinging from side to side as it searched the snowbanks below.

'Look!' she cried, pointing upwards. 'Some kind of hawk or eagle. That's probably the reason there are no rats. They're being hunted.'

'Analysis confirmed,' Walter droned, continuing with his computer game. 'Physical appearance of rodents necessitates nocturnal activity. Too conspicuous by day. Dark fur renders them easy prey for marauding predators.'

'Walter!' Joe growled.

'All right, all right,' he said placatingly. 'If it's serious you want, then how about this?'

Immediately a screen lit up on the cabin's back wall. It showed a carefully drawn contour map, with a range of mountains to the east, and a series of long slopes leading westward to an undulating plain.

'This is where we are now,' Walter explained, and an X appeared on the upper slopes of the mountains, just to the west of a high peak. 'And this is our route out of here.'

Without warning, the map tilted almost on edge,

becoming a recognisable landscape as it did so, and in a long swooping dive they entered it. Or that at least was how it felt, with the features of the landscape rushing towards them as they followed a projected path that plunged down through steep-sided gullies, skimmed across great swelling hillsides spiked with rocks, and plummeted into a narrow valley half blocked by tumbled boulders that threatened to halt their headlong rush at every turn.

Anna felt quite sick by the time the landscape levelled out and grew still.

'You're taking us down there?' she said incredulously, tearing her eyes from the now steady picture on the screen.

'Why not? Unless you can grow wings like that bird out there, it's the only way.'

'But how do you plan to do it?' Joe objected. 'This is a spaceship. It's not designed for overland travel. It doesn't have wheels, suspension, anything.'

'Aah, that'd be telling,' Walter replied, and chuckled secretively.

'So what's wrong with being open with us?'

'Well, it would spoil the surprise.'

'Surprise?' Anna looked despairingly at Joe. 'Are you asking us to trust you? Is that it?'

'I don't see why not,' Walter said, petulant again now. 'I had to take you two on trust, and you're nothing to write home about. Back on Titan, at the start of the project, all they'd tell me was that you'd be average, ordinary, run-of-the-mill.'

'They said that about *us*?' Joe responded.

'Well, what did you expect? All the real talent and brains are contained in those frozen embryos on the transports. You're just the parents, the minders, the Jacks-of-all-trades. Or Jill in your case, Anna. You had to be solid and dependable, that's all. Here, listen to what they say in your file: "Joseph Dugan. Slightly below average intelligence, but psychologically very stable. His limited abilities and lack of ambition make him an ideal candidate for the humdrum, day-to-day task of ...."'

'D'you know something, Walter?' Anna broke in coolly. 'For a clever person you can be really stupid sometimes.'

'Contradiction in terms,' Trog piped up from the sidelines.

While Og, triggered by his larger companion, added mysteriously: 'East is east and west is west and ne'er the twain shall meet.'

Nobody spoke much after that. For once Walter was diplomatic enough to withdraw; and Anna and Joe, feeling strangely glum, exchanged no more than a few words over breakfast. They had washed and dressed and were ready to go outside when Walter finally tried to make amends.

'Look,' he began awkwardly, in what Anna had already come to think of as his sorry-voice, 'I didn't mean anything. Honest. And all that business about a surprise – I just thought I'd give you a treat to make up for ...'

But they brushed aside his excuses. For the time being all they wanted was to be alone.

'Do whatever you please,' they told him as they stepped out into the sharply cold morning with its brilliant wash of sunlight.

'At least keep in radio contact,' he pleaded, and they ignored that too, trudging off across the snow to where the hillside dipped sharply downwards.

From there they had a clear view of the craggy, broken country below, and in the other direction, of a hazy peak still shrouded in mist. Even more important for the moment, they were well beyond Walter's hearing range.

Scooping the snow from a bulge of rock, they sat down with their backs turned pointedly towards the ship.

'So what did you make of that stuff about our files?' Anna asked.

Joe leaned over, formed his hand into a fist, and punched through the snow's brittle crust. 'They lied to us, didn't they?' he said bitterly. 'They told us we were special. The first parents!' He gave a hollow laugh. 'While all along we were just a couple of dummies. Boring old child-minders for their whizz kids in the transports.'

'Would you like to be a whizz kid?' she inquired. 'Like Walter, for instance?'

He pulled a face. 'God forbid!'

'Well then, there may be more important things than super intelligence. Things like loyalty and trust and courage – the sorts of qualities that make human life possible. And the people on Titan must have thought we possessed those qualities or they wouldn't have given us this job.'

'They still cheated us,' he insisted.

'True,' she agreed, 'but Titan's a long way off now.' She indicated the great vista of land falling away beneath them. 'This is *our* world, not theirs. We're the ones who count here. Who knows, being cleverer than everyone else may not count for much in a place like this. Courage and steadiness may count for a lot more.'

He looked at her curiously. 'Why d'you say that?'

'Look at the situation we're in. All those clever people back on Titan couldn't stop this happening;

and if you ask me we're going to need more than Walter's brilliance to get us through this in one piece.'

'I still don't see why,' he admitted.

She shrugged, unsure of how to express her sense of unease. 'Earth has changed. Don't ask me how exactly. It just has. I have this feeling about it. It's not the way they described it to us on Titan. Last night when I was fighting off the rats, I knew somehow that . . .'

She paused in mid-sentence as a shadow sped towards them across the snow and stopped almost at their feet. Startled, she and Joe both looked up together, to where one of the white birds hovered no more than two or three metres above their heads. At such close quarters they could see its hooked beak, and also the great taloned feet tucked away in the downy underside. Yet it was the eyes which most caught Anna's attention. For a split-second, as she stared into them, it was as if she were confronted once again by the knowing gaze of the rat. And with an involuntary cry she shielded her face and ducked down.

'What is it?' Joe asked, alarmed.

When there was no beating of wings about her head, she dared to look again and realised her mistake. Although these eyes possessed the same strange glint as the rat's, they were merely curious, with none of that furious quality which had so unnerved her the night before.

'It's just a bird,' Joe assured her. 'There's nothing to be scared of. Look, I'll show you.'

Reaching into his pocket he pulled out a biscuit, broke a piece off, and flung it into the air. Instantly the bird was upon it, its taloned foot closing so convulsively that the biscuit fractured into crumbs.

'More strength than brains,' Joe said with a laugh, and was about to pocket the remainder of the biscuit when something about the bird's eyes prompted Anna to reach out and take the fragment from him.

'Let's try again,' she said, and flung the biscuit up as before.

This time the bird caught it so delicately that not a single crumb spilled down.

'Hey, that's pretty smart,' Joe exclaimed, watching as the bird flew lazily away and landed on a nearby rock.

Like Anna, he expected the bird to feed hungrily. Instead, having inspected its find, it let out a shrill cry which rang loud and clear through the frosty air. Then, still clinging on to the biscuit, it took off and sailed further down the slope, where it was soon joined by others of its kind.

'What's it up to?' Joe asked.

'Let's take a look.'

Together they set off in pursuit, floundering through the deep snow and half tumbling down the steeper sections.

By the time they caught up it was clear to both of them that the birds were searching for something. But what? Some special place perhaps, for silently, now, they had begun circling a rocky outcrop, their eyes fixed intently upon it. It must have satisfied them because they soon rose higher, hovering there as if waiting. But again for what? Puzzled, Anna and Joe watched as just one of the birds peeled off from the rest, swept low, and dropped a tiny speck of something from its talons. The fragment of biscuit! Anna recognised it while it was still speeding downwards.

'What now?' Joe whispered.

The biscuit had landed on the snow some six or seven paces from the rocky outcrop, a tantalising distance which made Anna's heart lurch even before the first darkly whiskered face appeared in a gap between the rocks.

'Bait!' Joe breathed beside her. '*Rat* bait!'

Other rats now crowded into the gap, jostling together as though urging each other on. Their squeaks and squeals increased steadily, until one grey-brown animal, braver than the rest, burst from cover and scurried out across the snow.

Just as it reached the biscuit the first of the birds descended. In a flurry of snow and feathers the rat was bowled over and pinned helplessly. Yet not killed. Those spiked talons merely held it there, the bird standing over the terrified animal which called plaintively to its companions.

A whole group of rats broke from cover now, making not for the bait but for their common enemy. And that was when the rest of the birds struck. One by one they crashed into the advancing pack, birds and rats disappearing in glittering bursts of ice crystals.

Within seconds it was all over, the scuffed snow strewn with dead bodies. Letting out triumphant cries the birds snatched them up, their wingbeats slow and ponderous as they struggled clear of the slope and made off through the sparkling brightness of the morning.

'So Walter was right!' Joe exclaimed as the last of the rats was taken. 'The animals up here *have* evolved. The way those birds hunted together! It was the same as the rats last night. They've learned to organise themselves like ... like dogs or wolves. D'you remember the videos we were shown about

43

wolves and bees and . . . and ants – all those creatures programmed to co-operate? Well, this was exactly the same.'

But again Anna wasn't so sure. Some sixth sense warned her that the birds' method of attack had been more than just ant-like co-operation. It had been *too* carefully planned for that. The first bird, after all, had actually called the others together, and they in turn had played their parts perfectly, which surely suggested that there was a directing mind behind it all. Not one of the birds, but rather some kind of external force. An unknown presence that possessed an uncanny ability to work through simple animals and change their behaviour as it saw fit. But what could that force or presence be? Where was it hiding at this moment? And how had it possibly come by so much power?

She shook her head, no closer to the truth than before. 'I don't know,' she said doubtfully. 'I have this feeling we're up against more than evolution here. Something else is going on.'

'Any ideas?'

She pointed to a distant line of cliffs. 'That's where most of the birds flew to. Maybe we'll find our answer there.'

Again they followed the flight of the birds, this journey much longer than the last. To make the going easier they shared the lead, taking it in turns to break a passage through the thigh-deep snow; and for a while they made good time. Then, as they dipped into a shallow valley, they ran into head-high drifts that slowed them to a crawl. Soon, despite the freezing temperature, their faces were glistening with sweat. Yet at Anna's insistence they pressed on, and in the early afternoon they emerged onto a bony ridge swept almost clear of snow.

From there they had an unimpeded view of the cliffs some hundred metres away, and the first thing they noticed was the absence of the birds. There was no sign of them – no nests, no half-eaten bodies, nothing. The face of the cliffs, sheathed in ice, was utterly featureless, with not so much as a ledge for birds to roost on.

'Where could they have got to?' Anna began, and stopped as a bird seemed to step out of the cliff face and launch itself into the air.

She saw then what she had missed.

'Holes in the ice!' she cried, pointing. 'Look! There and there, lots of them. They must be entrances to caves.'

As if to illustrate her point a second bird appeared, its wingbeats pulsing overhead as it sped away.

'Birds living in caves?' Joe said wonderingly. 'I've never heard of that before.'

Nor had Anna. But what puzzled her more were the caves themselves. For the birds to use them as nesting sites, the caves first had to exist. So who had dug them out originally? And why? What exactly was at work in this harsh landscape, and what was its secret purpose?

More questions! That was all she seemed to encounter here. Never any answers. Or none that she could decipher.

'I think we'd better head back,' she said, feeling suddenly insecure. 'It's getting late.'

The sun by then was past its zenith, an extra chill already creeping into the air; and pursued by their own lengthening shadows they trudged off through the snow.

Following their outward trail they were able to make better time on the journey back, though still it was late in the afternoon when they laboured up the last slope.

For the previous hour or more they had been half expecting to run into Trog, sent out to find them, or to hear Walter's amplified voice calling through the silence of the day. But neither of those things had happened, and now, as they topped the final rise, they understood why. Walter, as well as Trog and Og, had been too busy. In the intervening hours they had done more than just work on the ship: they had transformed it.

It lay on its side as before. Now, however, it was sitting higher, supported by stout metal struts. Anna needed a moment or two to realise where they had come from. Yes, of course! The heat shields. They had been stripped away, and so had their metal supports, revealing the sleek lines of the ship's nose. Into that nose had been set a curved window which Anna recognised with a shock as the clear plastic cover of her own capsule.

Nor were these the only or even the most dramatic changes. At the rear of the ship the metal casing of the engines had also been stripped away. The longer sections of casing had been attached to the base of the supporting struts, rather like giant skis or runners. The rest had been fashioned into a huge fish-like tail that was hinged to the fuselage and clearly intended as a rudder.

'What's the verdict?' Walter greeted them as Anna and Joe laboured up the slope, his voice drifting out through the open airlock.

'It depends what it's supposed to be,' Joe answered.

Walter gave a 'humph' of disapproval. 'Isn't that obvious? Just look at it!'

'How about a sleigh?' Anna suggested.

'More than that,' he corrected her, his enthusiasm returning with a rush. 'It's a giant *bobsled!* You must have seen them on the old videos you were shown on Titan – those things that go zooming round icy bends at great speed. Well, this is my extra-special, hum-dinger, souped-up version. A little prod from the engines, that's all we'll need, and we'll be . . . *off*!' He blew a long tally-ho on a simulated trumpet. 'There'll be no stopping us. Snowdrifts and glaciers? No problem. Cliffs and walls of ice? A flick of the tail and we'll sail past. Hidden crevasses? You won't even know they're there, we'll be going so fast. With Captain Walter at the helm I'll have you off this mountain before you can say Jack Robinson.'

'You mean you're going to slide us all the way down on those . . . those *ski things*?' Joe broke in, indicating the makeshift runners beneath the ship.

'Why not?'

'Because it'll be *dangerous*. Have you seen the sort of country we have to get through? This is a *mountainside*, for God's sake!'

'Oh thou of little faith,' Walter droned in a mock-priestly voice.

'Even if we do get down in one piece, what then?' Anna added. 'A bobsled won't get us far once the snow runs out.'

'We'll think again,' he announced, switching back to his grand manner. 'Captain Walter, superbrain of the century, will come up with another of his amazing solutions.'

'And that's it?' she said incredulously. 'That's your master plan? For us to work out this journey one step at a time?'

'Two simultaneous steps impossible for bipeds,'

Trog commented, emerging from beneath the ship.

Og, his casing smeared with grease, chimed in with:
'Even the longest journey begins with one small step.'

Anna ignored them both. 'Well?' she challenged
Walter.

And from Joe: 'It's our lives you're playing with
here, Walter, remember that.'

Another disgruntled 'humph' floated out through
the airlock. 'Anyone listening to you two,' he complained, adopting his sulky tone, 'would think this
was a dangerous place. Well, I've got news for both
of you. It's not.'

'What about last night?'

'Is that all you're worried about?' he replied dismissively. 'A few measly rats? Pah! It was nothing. A
mere hiccup in the long breath of life; a bump in the
road to infinity; a ripple in the calm seas of creation;
a wisp of cloud in the eternal heavens; a ...' He
paused for imaginary breath and added: 'Listen, this
is your own true-blue planet, not some alien piece of
rock in outer space. This is Earth, the good old
World. In a word ... *Home*!' And with a chuckle he
broke into song:

> *Be it e-e-ver so hu-u-mble,*
> *There's n-o-o place like h-o-ome.*

'Or how about

> *Home is the hunter home from the hill*
> *And the sailor is home from the sea.*

'Then again there're all those old sayings, like
"Home is where the heart is" and "Charity begins
at home" and ...'

While he babbled happily on, Anna turned and gazed out over the now dusky landscape. Was Walter right? Was this simply 'home'? The known, dependable planet that had nurtured her ancestors for millennia? With most of its large animals wiped out centuries earlier, during the crisis, was it now safer than ever, as she had been led to believe? As Walter *still* believed?

She hoped so.

On the other hand something about the place continued to nag at her. In an indefinable way it had changed. She could almost sense the difference in the encroaching shadows. There was, she suspected, a wholly new factor at work here: a secret, hidden thing which, as yet, they had no real idea of.

5

Walter roused them in the early dawn.

'Rise and shine! Shake a leg!' he announced in his captain's voice. 'There's a whole new world waiting for us out there.'

Anna groaned and opened her eyes. She had slept only fitfully, troubled by thoughts of what lay ahead; but then she noticed tiny footprints on the outer surface of the ship's new windshield and she didn't feel so bad about leaving. Anything was better than staying there and having rats peer in at her while she slept.

'Look lively, my hearties,' Walter urged them as she and Joe dressed and wolfed down a simple breakfast. 'Time and tide wait for no man.'

'Mountains unaffected by tides,' Trog pointed out in his precise way.

Og, as usual, joined in with: 'There is a tide in the affairs of men which, taken at the flood, leads on to fortune.'

'Get aft, the pair of you!' Walter bawled in his best imitation of a pirate captain, and they scurried off to work the makeshift rudder they had rigged up on the previous day.

Anna and Joe, with nothing else to do, stationed themselves at the front window.

'Prepare to cast off,' Walter warned them, and just as the sun peeped above the far horizon the engines purred into life and nudged them forward.

That first small thrust was all they needed. Once set upon the downward slope the ship's own momentum did the rest, carrying them effortlessly over the hard-packed snow.

'Not bad, hey?' Walter commented with a chuckle.

For a while at least Anna had to admit that it really was quite pleasant to sit there watching the snow-fields slip past. Then, as the ship gathered speed, she began to feel less relaxed.

'Shouldn't we slow down?' she asked, trying not to sound as scared as she felt.

'Slow down?' Walter replied recklessly. 'What for? Remember the old saying, Anna – faint heart never won fair land.'

'Fair lady,' Og corrected him from somewhere rear of the main cabin.

'I think Anna's right,' Joe added nervously, clinging onto his seat as the ship swung around a yawning chasm. 'This is way too fast. You should use the brakes.'

'Brakes?' Walter let out a long peal of derisive laughter. 'What brakes? This is a giant bobsled, not a kiddy-car.'

'D'you mean . . .?' Anna and Joe began together, but before they could finish, the ship plunged into a steeply spiralling valley.

All they could do was hold on after that, with the ship swinging sideways as it careered around the first bend. Other bends followed, some so tight that they were in danger of riding up over the valley's rim.

'We're not going to make it!' Joe shouted as a boulder loomed into their path, but somehow they skimmed past and entered a narrow gully that fell away more steeply than ever.

The ship was groaning now under the strain, its makeshift runners clattering noisily, yet Walter seemed not to notice. Even Anna and Joe's growing terror had no effect on him.

'Ride 'im, cowboy!' he yelled, happily mixing up his games.

In a shower of ice and snow they cleared a heap of rocks and landed with a jolt that knocked Anna from her seat. She scrambled up in time to glimpse another rocky outcrop sailing past beneath them.

Beneath them?

There was an eerie silence, with just the wind singing past the hull. Then once again they crashed down, with such force that both Anna and Joe were sent rolling across the cabin floor.

Braced against the back wall, they watched in horror as the narrow twisting gully rushed to meet them, its snow-encrusted walls reduced to a blur.

'You've got to stop this thing!' Joe yelled above the noise and juddering vibration.

'Can't be done,' Walter replied shortly.

Even he sounded less confident now. And with good reason, for less than halfway down the gully, unable to take a particularly tight bend, the ship grazed the rocky wall. There was a shriek of tortured metal and they veered away, scraping the opposite wall and yawing dangerously.

'All under control,' Walter assured them, slewing the craft back on course.

A few seconds later, however, they were in trouble again. Approaching the lower end of the gully at dizzying speed, they shot through the narrow opening and arced out into space. For a few agonising seconds the same eerie silence as before completely enveloped them, except that this time the landing was like a massive fist slamming into the underside of the ship. Two of the side ports burst outwards with a ping of shattered glass; and something cracked beneath them, causing the whole ship to heel over and weave drunkenly. To make matters worse they had landed on the half-shattered remains of an ancient glacier. Like some crazy highway, blackened by scree and strewn with jagged teeth of ice, it stretched away into the mist below, seemingly impassable.

Anna, who had clawed her way back into her seat, took one horrified look and closed her eyes in terror.

'Get us out of here, Walter!' she wailed, her voice rising above the clatter of the shuddering craft.

'I'm doing my best . . .' he began, and was cut short by a jarring thump as the ship crashed against an icy boulder and bounced off. '. . . do-oing m-y-y be-est to kee-eep us-s-s in one p-pie-iece . . . ' he continued in a strangely uncertain voice, and was again interrupted by a great thump and the scream of tearing metal.

'Walter!' she shouted. 'What's happening to you?'

There was no answer. And for Anna and Joe that was the worst part, with the ship completely out of control now, the noise of their descent almost deafening. Thump after thump followed, each collision racketing them from one side of the cabin to the other. Pummelled and bruised, they hung on as best they could to chairs or fittings, but the next impact would shake them loose, their desperate cries drowned out by the general din.

By then the whole ship seemed to be screaming out in protest. The undercarriage had all but collapsed, bringing it into direct contact with the icy surface; the already battered sides were growing ever more buckled and creased as the ship charged along; and what was left of the ports were blowing out one by one, allowing the shriek of the wind to fill the cabin.

It was that constant noise of wind which Anna found most unnerving. Jammed at last in the narrow section of the nose-cone, she covered her ears with both hands, trying to block it out. But with each fresh jolt she had to grab for a handhold, and the noise was back, going on and on until she felt it would never end.

She didn't actually hear it stop. A sudden blow on the head left her slightly groggy, and when her mind cleared, the ship had come to rest and surprisingly warm air was blowing in through the nearest port. Yet it was the silence she was most thankful for – that and the sight of Joe stirring in the far corner. He had a cut over one eye and a bruise already blossoming along the line of his jaw, but otherwise he seemed unharmed.

'You okay?' she asked shakily.

'I think so,' he said, and gave her a rueful grin just as Trog and Og appeared in the far doorway and trotted briskly down the sloping floor of the cabin.

'Abandon ship,' Trog declared, punching the manual switch on the airlock, which creaked open.

'Women and children first,' Og added, and stepped clear of the opening, to make way for the living members of the crew.

Hazily Anna wondered what they were up to. The decision to abandon ship, after all, was only supposed to be taken in the event of something happening to . . .

She sat up so abruptly that she cracked her head again, making her ears ring.

'Walter?' she cried, alarmed by the very silence she had welcomed only seconds earlier. 'Can you still hear me?'

It was Trog, in a sense, who gave her the answer she dreaded.

'Regulation 2463/7/ii,' he droned, 'states that when ship ceases to function, all personnel should leave forthwith.'

'Get out while you're ahead,' Og agreed readily.

'We've lost him,' Joe whispered, putting into words her deepest fear. 'He must be dead.'

Dead, she knew, was the wrong term for someone like Walter; and yet at that moment it seemed all too appropriate.

'Gone?' she queried, listening still for that childlike voice she had so quickly grown used to. 'Have we really lost him? I can hardly believe it.'

But although she went on sitting there, waiting, no familiar voice seeped from the cabin walls. There was a lurch, that was all, as the ship settled, and suddenly she found herself on the verge of tears.

'Damn you, Walter!' she broke out, though her anger was directed at herself, not at him. 'I should never have let you talk us into this.'

The ship lurched again and seemed to sigh, as if giving up the ghost, and her tears flooded down.

'Hey!' Joe was bending over her. 'Don't get upset. He was a machine, nothing else.'

Was that all he'd been? Just a machine? she asked herself, and knew he hadn't. The expression on Joe's face suggested that despite his words he felt the same. For both of them, Walter had become a living being; an unruly, inventive, sometimes impossible companion, but a companion for all that.

'Crew now in contravention of above-mentioned

regulation,' Trog reminded them.

'Oh go to hell, Trog,' she replied miserably, wiping her eyes and staggering to her feet.

'Place in question purely mythological,' he responded. 'Cannot be accessed in real world.'

'The road to hell is paved with good intentions,' Og contributed for good measure.

Ignoring the transformers, Anna and Joe limped from the silent ship. That wasn't an easy thing to do, like turning their backs on someone dear to them; but as they both reluctantly admitted, there was no further reason to stay. With Walter gone, the ship was a dead thing, useless except as a temporary shelter. Their future lay outside, in the wider world, which greeted them with a searing blaze of sunlight.

From the vantage point of a small hillock, they surveyed their present situation. Behind them lay the mountain, a series of towering buttresses built of rock, ice and snow, and topped by a jagged peak. How they had managed to descend from *that* and still be in one piece, they couldn't imagine. And yet thanks to Walter, here they were, safe.

'I'm going to miss him,' Anna admitted in a choked voice, and stared mistily out over the undulating plain that awaited them.

As far as she could see there was nothing but desert. A little scrub grew from the parched soil close at hand, but within a kilometre or two it petered out, giving way to rolling sand dunes. The mountain had been daunting enough, but this wasteland was even worse. Devoid of life, growth, water, it stood like an unbridgeable gulf between them and the distant transports. Without Walter's help it would clearly be impossible to cross.

56

Despairingly, they turned their attention to the ship. It was a sorry sight. Lying at an angle, its nose sunk into a drift of sand, it looked more like a junk-yard version of their once splendid craft. Its sides were torn and crumpled, its ports gone, as were most of its runners and supports; and most devastating of all, one of its two massive engines had been ripped from the fuselage and lay abandoned on a nearby slope. Of the tail-like steering device rigged up the day before, only a few tattered sheets of metal cladding remained.

'What a mess!' Joe groaned. 'We'll never get out of here now.'

'It may not be as bad as it looks,' Anna offered hopefully.

Joe shook his head. 'It's probably worse. No wonder Walter didn't survive. Though maybe that's just as well. I'm not sure even he could have got this heap moving again.'

Anna had no stomach for that kind of speculation – it only made her loss harder to bear.

'So all we have left are the transformers,' she said sadly, indicating the two stocky figures at her side. 'D'you think they can get us across this desert?'

'Not in their present condition. They'd probably creak to a halt in the sand. We'd have to modify them, and for that we'd need ...'

'Modification of transformers forbidden in absence of higher authority,' Trog interrupted promptly. 'I refer you to regulation 1793/1/i.'

And Og, much more direct: 'Keep your thieving hands off me.'

'I was just saying,' Joe continued with heavy emphasis, 'that we couldn't begin to modify them without Walter's help. He was the key to everything.'

Anna nodded. Everything came back to Walter. And now that he . . . now . . .

There was a familiar prickle at the backs of her eyes, and she was about to turn tearfully away when she heard something. A faint stirring or rustling of a kind she had heard once before. But when? And more to the point, where was it coming from now? The scrubby undergrowth perhaps?

Mindful of the dangers they had encountered on the mountain, she whirled around, her eyes searching amongst the stunted trees that hugged the lower portion of the hillock on which she stood. Was that a slight movement she could see? No, it was merely the wind disturbing the tinder-dry foliage. In any case the noise had surely come from somewhere else.

The same faint rustling occurred again, behind her, and she whirled back and took a first tentative step towards the ship.

'It's just the heavy tail section settling into the sand,' Joe assured her, but she wasn't convinced.

'Listen!' she hissed.

And with their ears straining for the least sound, they heard it. The feeblest of whispers, which they might have mistaken for the passing breeze had it not been for the underlying suggestion of words.

'. . . w-w-wha' h-h-h-hi-hi' m-m-me . . .? W-w-wh-wh-o-o t-t-tur-ur-urn ou-ou' l-l-igh-igh's-s-s?'

There was no mistake now. It was definitely coming from the battered opening to the airlock.

'Is that really you, Walter?' Anna whispered, hardly daring to hope.

The reply was a little louder, firmer, but hardly less confused '. . . c-c-can' s-s-seem t-to . . . CLICK . . . can' s-seem to . . . CLICK . . . can' seem to f-focus . . . CLICK . . . focus . . . CLICK . . . focus . . .'

'Walter!' Anna and Joe burst out together, and made a dash for the ramp.

'Regulation 2463/7/ii no longer applies,' Trog commented, trotting along behind; while Og satisfied himself with: 'Back to square one.'

Once inside the ship Joe knocked lightly on the curved wall. 'Walter, can you hear us?'

'H-hear you . . . CLICK . . . hear you . . . CLICK . . . l-loud and . . . CLICK . . . loud and clear-learlearlearlearlearlearlearlear . . .'

'Can you still function?' Anna added.

'Usessless . . . ulessess . . . ulseeses . . . usessell . . . uselessessessess . . .' the voice replied, struggling repeatedly with the word. And then 'N-need time . . . CLICK . . . time to reagonise . . . CLICK . . . reor-nigise . . . CLICK . . . reorganise damned circuses . . . CLICK . . . dam-dam-damaged circles . . . cycles . . . CLICK . . . damaged cir-cir-circuits . . .'

'How long do you need?'

'H-hard to sing . . . song . . . sag . . . CLICK . . . hard to say . . . CLICK . . . must hose gown . . . dose clown . . . CLICK . . . must close down now.'

The cabin immediately grew still, the atmosphere strangely unresonant, soundless except for the warm desert breeze humming through the shattered ports.

Joe looked questioningly at Anna. 'Do you think he'll make it? You know, get himself back together?'

'He did before, after the shields failed.'

'Yes, but this is different. He's taken a terrible pounding.'

Anna shrugged, acting much calmer than she felt. 'We can only wait and see. At least he's alive. That's something.'

For once it was Og alone who broke into the

conversation. 'Where there's life there's hope,' he chirruped brightly.

But surrounded by the battered craft, and having just heard Walter's jumbled attempts at speech, neither Anna nor Joe felt nearly so confident.

6

Anna had the eerie sensation that she was being watched; that invisible eyes were probing the darkness, searching her out. It couldn't be Walter, who was still in a state of withdrawal after nearly twelve hours. Nor was it Joe whose steady breaths right there beside her meant that he was still fast asleep. Who then?

She sat up in the pitch dark, taking care not to disturb Joe. Clearly she was either imagining things or some unknown creature had managed to creep into the ship during the night. But how could it have got in? With the help of the transformers they had blocked off all the ports; and although there were numerous holes in the hull, according to Trog's sensors none came right through to the cabin.

It had to be her imagination then, she decided ... and hesitated. Or did it? Try as she might, she couldn't shake off the feeling that something was there in the cabin with them. Furtively she reached for the emergency lamp left lying beside the capsule.

Clicking it on, she swung the beam around the walls. Nothing! Except of course for Trog's eyes gazing dully from the cavity. Was it perhaps he that she had sensed? She shook her head. No, she thought of him more as a part of the ship itself. Something else had to be ...

A tiny 'peep' made her direct the lamp at the ceiling, swinging the beam so rapidly to and fro that she nearly missed it: a creature as small and insignificant as the sound she had just heard. It was clinging to the ceiling immediately overhead – a frail lizard-like animal with sucker feet and round out-sized eyes that were fixed on her upturned face. It looked extraordinarily gentle until she noticed the moth clamped in its jaws. The insect was still alive, its wings fluttering feebly; but then the jaws chomped down hard, the neck arched, and the moth was gone, swallowed whole. Next, with a suddenness that made Anna jump, a long grey-black tongue darted out and licked around the creature's muzzle, sliding easily over the bulging surface of the eyes.

Joe stirred beside her. 'Wazzamatta?' he mumbled, blinking sleepily in the wash of lamplight.

She pointed upwards, keeping the beam centred on the lizard-like animal.

'Oh that,' he said dismissively, sinking back onto the pillow. 'It's one of those what-d'you-call-thems.' He needed a few seconds to hunt out the name. 'Geckos. That's it, a gecko. They're common in the warm parts of Earth, including deserts. That's what it said in the natural history program we had to study, anyway.'

'Are they ... dangerous?' she asked, unnerved by those watchful eyes.

'No, they often used to live in people's houses. They're completely harmless. Here, take a look.' Reaching up, he flicked one hand at the ceiling. 'Shoo! Go on, get out of here.'

But like the rat Anna had encountered on the

snow, the gecko held its ground. Its only response to Joe's threat was to let out another of its peeping cries, and more of its kind scuttled out from nooks and crannies all over the cabin.

With a small cry of her own, Anna leaped clear of the capsule and fumbled with the lamp, clicking it onto wide beam. As its light flooded the surrounding space she saw that some twenty or thirty of the geckos had grouped into a tightly packed circle on the ceiling – the self-same defensive pattern that the rats had formed.

'Whatever's going on here,' she said in a shaky voice, 'I don't like it.'

Even Joe seemed less sure of himself. 'That's odd,' he said, scratching his head. 'I seem to remember they were loners, not group animals. Still, there's not much they can do to hurt us.' And he was about to shoo them away for the second time when Anna stopped him.

'No, leave them!' she barked out. 'Just in case. Let Trog do it.'

The mere mention of his name was enough to bring Trog tumbling out of the cavity.

'Unwanted passengers on board,' he intoned.

'Yes, we know. Get rid of them for us. Anyway you please.'

'Most indigenous species fear fire,' he informed them, and one of his hands flipped over to reveal a blowlamp fixture.

It ignited with a dull roar, and he pointed it upwards, sending the geckos streaming across the ceiling. He followed, playing the flames to and fro in their wake, herding them towards the nearest port where they slipped out into the night.

'Ship now clear,' he reported. 'Unwanted species

have returned to their natural habitat.'

'Dragging their tails behind them,' a muffled voice added from the region of Trog's chest.

'But how did they get in here in the first place?' Anna asked, puzzled. 'I could have sworn we sealed that port.'

'So could I,' Joe agreed.

'Assumption correct,' Trog said. 'Repairs have since been modified by unknown agent.'

'Modified?' Lamp in hand, Anna approached the port for a closer look. Sure enough, wedged between the inner wall and the piece of plastic they had clamped over the opening was a length of twig. The gap it created was hardly more than a crack, but still big enough for a gecko to squeeze through.

'Look at this,' she said. 'They didn't get in by themselves. Someone's helping them, organising them. Just like the rats.'

'Present assumption carries a probability factor of only 0.35,' Trog replied dispassionately. 'Other poss . . .'

'Never mind your other possibilities,' she broke in. 'Just do your job. Make this place secure.'

Again the blowlamp roared into life, burning away the intrusive piece of twig and allowing the cover to snap back against the inner wall.

That last burst of heat, however, had a very different effect on the rest of the ship. A shudder seemed to pass through the hull, and a drawling, uncertain voice declared:

'Fireman hot steam. Corruption: Fire on the port team . . . ream . . . beam.' A piercing whistle, like feedback from a microphone, drowned out everything for a few moments, and then: 'As you worm. I deplete, fine downy pillow. Amen . . . I mean, Fire down pillow . . . billow . . . below. Which rewinds me, Hello. How argue? Hop your doomwell. Arm brewing fine.'

Anna turned to Joe in consternation. The voice itself was Walter's – still young and unformed – but it seemed to have regressed further and to be struggling with the very rudiments of language.

She took a deep breath and said as calmly as she could: 'How do you feel, Walter?'

'Bleeding spot . . . bloody knot . . . cot . . . hot,' he faltered out, and broke into uneven laughter as though he were enjoying himself. 'Worms lick daughter . . . Corruption: Words lick . . . like wa-wa-water. Kip flipping off tong. Too hurd . . . hard fur Halter . . . fur Wal-wal-wallie.'

She nodded, more or less following what he was trying to say.

'What about your functions?' Joe asked. 'Are they working now?'

'Elsie stems flow,' he began, gave a soft chuckle and tried again. 'Elsie stems go.'

'All systems go?' Anna queried.

'Connect.' And to show what he meant he switched on the main lights and restarted the air-conditioning unit, a wash of cool air sweeping through the cabin. 'Distaff eel cod?'

'Does that feel good?' Anna repeated, and smiled for the first time since setting out from the mountaintop. 'Yes it does, very good. But what else can you do, Walter? How about getting us out of here? Is that possible?'

'Go goblin,' he replied promptly, and corrected that with: 'No gobbling . . . hobbling . . . wobbling . . . Ah, blurry well!' Then with a final effort: 'No pro-pro-problem.'

65

'So you really can get us across the desert?' Joe pressed him.

'Easter fallen off lock.'

'Easier than falling off a log,' Anna explained – unnecessarily, because she could see from Joe's broad grin that he had already understood.

'So how do you plan to go about it, Walter? I mean, no offence, but the ship's really in a mess.'

'Weather swill this way.'

'What?'

'Where there's a will there's a way,' Og's muffled voice explained, and with a soft clang he unfolded himself from Trog and stood beside his companion.

'Looks as though we're in for another of Walter's surprises,' Anna commented softly, but evidently there was nothing wrong with his hearing.

'Surplus! Surplus!' he confirmed.

'And that's all you're going to tell us?'

'Auctions spick larder downwards,' he replied mysteriously.

'Actions speak louder than words,' Og added, and as if to prove the point, both Trog and Og made resolutely for the airlock.

'Stage one of reconstruction about to begin,' Trog announced as he stepped out into the breaking dawn.

'Hi ho, hi ho, it's off to work we go,' Og chanted, following him down the ramp.

Anna and Joe remained behind for a while, trying unsuccessfully to coax more information out of Walter. Yet although unusually quiet, he was obliging enough, supplying them with their first hot meal in twenty-four hours, and even turning on the water in the aft cabin, so they could have a much needed shower. Equally important, he seemed oddly cheerful, as if their recent catastrophe had left him feeling carefree. More than once, while they were showering and eating breakfast, they were aware of a low background hum. It puzzled them for a while, until Anna suddenly realised what it was.

'He's singing,' she whispered. 'Listen.'

It was true. The gentle rise and fall of sound contained faint hints of melody, like a child's first groping attempts at song.

He was still humming softly to himself when they went out to inspect the work on the ship. To their surprise it was already well advanced, Og and Trog between them having repaired all the tears in the hull. Now they were busy staggering down the hillside with the severed engine, their sturdy legs sinking knee-deep into the sand.

They didn't re-attach it straight away. First they had to raise and level the ship, which they did by using the hydraulic strength of their own limbs. With a 'One, two, three, go,' from Og, they heaved it up, the sand pouring from its buried nose, and set it upon prepared columns of stone. That done, they straightened and repositioned the few remaining struts; then, with curved strips of metal scavenged from the tail section, they fitted new skis or runners.

'Oh no,' Joe groaned, looking on in consternation, 'not another bobsled! What's the use of it down here, where there're no hills?'

But he needn't have worried, for with the ship firmly seated upon its new runners, Og and Trog now set about remounting the severed engine. Except that this time, instead of facing it fore and aft, they bolted and welded it crosswise to the hull.

'What are they up to now?' Anna wondered aloud as they disappeared into the cabin and began cutting and hacking in there.

They emerged some minutes later with strips of rubberised flooring which they formed into two continuous loops. These were pushed through prepared holes in the engine casing and attached to the mysterious inner workings, the loose ends of the loops dangling free.

At that point both transformers seemed to take leave of their senses – as far as Anna and Joe were concerned anyway – because they clambered up the sides of the ship and began cutting into the hull.

'I can't go on watching this,' Joe said in a worried voice, and stomped off through the scrub.

Anna found him a few minutes later sitting in the speckled shade of some stunted desert trees, their frond-like leaves making paper rustlings in the breeze. He was looking at the ground in what she thought was a state of despondency, until she followed his gaze and noticed the network of markings there. Fashioned from clay, they could best be described as a series of raised lines which crisscrossed each other in a weirdly intricate pattern.

'What are those?' she asked.

Joe patted the ground beside him. 'Just watch and you'll see.'

She didn't have long to wait. At one of the junctions of the intersecting lines, a tiny trapdoor flew up and the head of a gecko appeared. With Anna and Joe sitting stock still, it showed no signs of alarm; and seconds later, as if some secret signal had been given, other trapdoors opened elsewhere in the pattern. Not many geckos actually emerged, and it soon became clear why. The raised lines were a system of tunnels connecting the various nests. The whole thing, as far as Anna could judge, was a beautifully designed gecko colony.

'You're not going to tell me they could have worked all that out for themselves,' she said softly, careful not to alarm the gecko sentries.

Joe gave the faintest of shrugs. 'Termites can do it,' he pointed out. 'You've seen those holograms of termite mounds.'

'Yes, but termites are hot-wired for this sort of thing. They've taken millions of years to evolve.'

'Maybe geckos have evolved too, while we've been away.'

She shook her head. 'They haven't had long enough. Like I said before, there's someone or something behind all this. It's a bit like watching Trog and Og. They *seem* to be intelligent until you realise they're just obeying instructions. The fact is, unless we tell them what to do, they're pretty useless.'

'Who is this someone then?' Joe queried, looking straight at her. 'This person who's arranging everything behind the scenes?'

But she still had no answer to that.

'It would have to be a kind of god, wouldn't it?' he pressed her. 'To affect the rats and the birds, and even these little creatures down here?'

A kind of god? She thought about the idea and dismissed it uneasily.

'No, not a god. Just someone who believes they're god. I was thinking more along the lines of a super version of Walter.'

'Someone else would still have had to make him,' Joe insisted.

'Yeah, that's the problem.'

It was a problem that continued to confront them as they wandered off through the desert scrub, for wherever they looked they saw examples of order and design. The small finch-like birds that flitted through

69

the sparse foliage didn't simply fly away at the sight
of human intruders. They gathered first into a
defensive flock and then retreated to drop-like clusters of woven nests set in the topmost branches of
the trees.

The same ordered activity was apparent in other
ground animals and birds. The darting, lean-bodied
skinks, the spring-tailed wrens, the tiny feral mice,
the larger blue-headed lizards – all had gathered into
colonies and built for themselves weirdly beautiful
dwellings.

Baffled and also entranced by what they saw, Anna
and Joe were finally driven back to the ship by the
mounting heat of the day. By then, hungry and
thirsty as well as hot, they looked forward to relaxing
in the air-conditioned comfort of the cabin. Which
was why their first sight of the ship came as such a
shock.

Gone was their secure, self-contained retreat. In
their absence a great hole had been cut in the top of
the roof. Over this opening, like a giant sunshade,
was stretched an awning made from the insulating
material that had lined the hull. As for that part of
the roof which had been cut away – the metal plates
had since been refashioned into something that
looked suspiciously like a paddlewheel. Fastened to
the tail section of the ship and resting on the sand,
it was connected to the remounted engine by the two
loops of rubberised belt. With the damaged engine
slowly turning over, the belts, plainly enough, would
drive the paddlewheel round and round, scooping at
the sand and propelling the ship forward on its
runners.

Or that at least was the plan. The big question was
whether it would work.

'It ... it looks like one of those old steamboats!'
Joe broke out, gazing at it in astonishment. 'Here we
are in a desert, not a drop of water to be seen, and
Walter decides to build us a boat! A paddlewheeler!
Has he gone crazy or something?'

'No evidence of mental instability,' Trog responded, emerging from the underside of the ship
where he had been tinkering with the makeshift steering gear.

And Og: 'No Mad Hatters for us.'

Followed by the two transformers, Anna and Joe
re-entered the ship. The cabin, as they had feared,
was barely recognisable: its floor stripped to the bare
metal; its roof gone, replaced by the awning which
billowed and rippled in the hot afternoon breeze. It
seemed that the only thing which hadn't changed was
Walter, who continued to sing softly to himself as
though delighted with his handiwork.

'Walter!' Anna said sternly, not quite knowing
whether to gaze at the bare floor or the truncated
walls. 'Is this the best you can do?'

'The hairy vest,' he affirmed.

'What?'

'The very best,' Og translated.

'So you honestly think this will get us across the
desert?'

'Probability of success ...' Trog began, but Anna
cut him short.

'I'm talking to Walter,' she insisted. 'Well, will it
get us out of here?'

'Popes toes,' he replied.

'You hope so?'

'Connect.'

'And if it doesn't?'

'Wall bed ... all fed ... dead,' he answered, and

71

sighed, though not nearly as sadly as she might have expected.

'Well, if we're going to give it a try,' Joe said resolutely, 'let's make a start. We're ready if you are.'

'Rot wet ... not set ... yet,' he responded. 'Poo pot ... Corruption: too knot ... h-hot ... CLICK ... Angie ... energy ... eng-eng-engine might oven eat.'

'You mean the engine could overheat?'

'Eggs act ... exact tree ... exactly.'

'When should we leave then?'

'Rafter dust.'

'Say that again. I didn't get it.'

'After dusk,' Trog explained.

'When heavenly shades of night are falling,' Og added.

'Okay,' Anna agreed. 'But just one more thing. Where are we making for? Tonight, I mean.'

Instead of answering her in words, Walter lit up a screen set into the wall. It showed a portion of the Earth's surface photographed from outer space. Then the camera lens zoomed in, revealing an almost featureless desert bordered on one side by the characteristic folds of a mountain range, and on the other by a glittering expanse of sea. An X appeared at the inner edge of the desert, to show where they were, and the camera zoomed in closer still, following the progress of a dotted line that snaked across the plain towards their immediate destination – the one small green spot in a sea of sand.

'What's that?' Joe asked, pressing his finger to the screen.

'Os-os-osiris ...' Walter stuttered out. 'Corruption: Assissi ... oar sizes ... oar aces ...'

'He means an oasi ...' Og began.

72

'No,' Anna interrupted. 'Let him say it for himself.'

He fetched a deep sigh and tried again: 'Oar seizes ... oast houses ... ooze hazes ...' And then, with unusual clarity: 'I fad a snuff! Jest cool it Eden.'

'Eden?' Anna asked sharply. 'Why do you call it that?'

He refused to speak again, however, reverting to his half-melodic song – humming it softly to himself for the remainder of the day.

7

Evening shadows were already staining the lower
slopes of the mountain by the time they set out.

'Sandfly to carthorse,' Walter warned them. And
when they failed to react, gazing at the walls with
puzzled expressions: 'Sandbar ... Stand bar ...
by ... to cast aft ... off.'

From the rear of the ship there came a low throb
as the engine started, followed by a grinding rumble
as the twin belts engaged and the paddlewheel began
scooping at the sand. With a jolt they were in motion,
sliding jerkily into a hollow and then up over the first
sandy crest.

'Seer west slowest, Mister Question,' Walter bel-
lowed in something of his old pirate captain manner.

'What was that?' Anna asked, having to raise her
voice above the steady grind and roar of the
paddlewheel.

'I think he's telling Trog to steer west by south-
west,' Joe answered, and jerked his thumb towards
the rear cabin where Trog was handling the steering
gear.

'Got it in one,' Og commented.

Og was struggling to keep his balance on the
swaying deck, and as the ship plunged into an unusually deep hollow he lost his footing altogether and

went cartwheeling down towards the nose-cone.

'Show yourself mating,' Walter instructed him.

'What?' Anna and Joe shared startled glances.

The answer issued from somewhere amongst Og's jumbled limbs. 'He's telling me to stow myself away,' he said, and converting into a four-legged creature he crabbed his way back up the deck.

'What about the mating part?'

Og obediently folded himself into Trog's chest. 'He means naval rating, another word for sailor,' came the muffled reply.

'Oh!' And for the first time in hours, Anna and Joe burst out laughing – partly at the feeble joke, but mainly out of sheer relief at being under way at last. For already one thing was clear: Walter's chosen method of crossing the desert, although uncomfortable and noisy, was proving surprisingly effective, the shadowy stretches of sand and scrub sliding by at twenty to thirty kilometres an hour.

With the coming of dark they left most of the scrub behind, and after that their progress was much smoother, the ship pitching gently to and fro as it rode the swelling sand dunes. They would have been almost comfortable if it hadn't been for the grit which filled the air now that the wind had dropped. Kicked up in great clouds by the steady grinding of the paddlewheel, most of it fell in their wake, but still enough eddied in under the awning to make life difficult. Even Walter was affected by it.

'Id ... witches ... hitches ... itches,' he complained.

Anna and Joe both agreed, the dust irritating their eyes.

Yet for Walter, as they were soon to realise, the flying dust was altogether more serious, finding its

75

way into his already damaged circuits and shorting them out.

The first indication of this new hazard was when all the lights on board suddenly clicked off. Seconds later one of the storage compartments clattered open, spilling an assortment of tools and cooking utensils onto the deck.

'What's happening?' Anna cried.

'Circuses paying up,' he explained. 'Too much rust in the lair.'

'Can't you get rid of it? Blow it out of your system or something?'

'O year!' he agreed enthusiastically. 'Lair positioning ... commissioning ... conditioning to the rest cure.'

While Anna was still working out what he meant, a cloud of dust billowed from the vents as the air-conditioning unit set about scouring the hull clean.

'Aah, dads butter,' he sighed. And then clearer still: 'Nutting like a good keening. I fill like a new maid ... omigosh! ... man.'

Evidently it wasn't only his speech that he had improved slightly, but also his sense of melody, for he immediately began to croon a familiar tune to the words 'Starry barry light'.

'What's he on about now?' Joe asked.

Anna looked up through the windscreen. The Milky Way, like a great glittering river, arched majestically above them.

'I think he's enjoying the night sky,' she said.

'The bluest words you ever stroke,' Walter agreed with a chuckle. 'Rook addict ... at it. The grace of cod ... Corrossion: The face of ... of good.'

'Are you serious?' Joe queried, intrigued by his last remark.

But Walter was too engrossed in the heavens even to answer.

'Window full,' he sighed, and broke into a wordless song that seemed to reach out, almost welcoming, into the surrounding night, weaving a strange aura of peace around the ship as it trundled noisily along.

Anna, as entranced by the song as by the night itself, felt all her anxieties about the journey begin to slip away.

'Just think,' she said dreamily, peering ahead at the lines of oncoming dunes, 'once, long ago, camels would have carried people across this desert. People who'd never heard a radio; who'd never even read a book; who believed the stars were living things, just like themselves.'

'What made you think of them?' Joe murmured.

She gestured vaguely to the star-silvered landscape. 'I'm not sure if I'm making this up or not, but I half remember reading once how camel drivers sang to their animals to keep them going.'

'Is that how you think of Walter's song?' Joe asked, studying her curiously. 'As keeping *us* going?'

'In a way. Right now, while he's singing like this, he seems to be a part of this place and of everything that went before. It's as if . . . as if . . .'

But as with Walter, words failed her when she needed them most, and she drifted off into silence, lulled by the song and by the eerie beauty of the desert.

She hadn't expected to sleep, what with the dust and the noise from the churning paddlewheel. So she was both surprised and pleased, many hours later, to find herself being gently woken by Og.

'Awake!' he announced grandly. 'For morning in

77

the bowl of night/Hath flung the stone that sets the stars to flight.'

'Wha . . .?' she muttered, hearing only a jumble of words.

'He means it's nearly time for breakfast,' Joe explained.

She sat up, shivering in the chilly grey dawn, the sky behind them already a blaze of pinkish light. On either hand the russet colours of the desert were slowly emerging from the dark, but it was the splash of bright green straight ahead which caught her attention.

'Is that Eden?' she said aloud. 'How long before we get there?'

'Doughnut count your chicklins before they hashed,' Walter warned her seriously.

She detected then the acrid smell of burning, and she peered beneath the awning to see a thin trail of smoke rising from the cross-mounted engine.

'The engine's been overheated like that for an hour or more,' Joe explained. 'It's why we're going so slowly.'

'Slow but steady wins the race,' Og commented as he handed them each a warm drink.

Cups in hand, they sipped absently at their drinks, watching with anxious eyes as the ship crawled its way across the dunes. During its descent into the shadowy troughs it would speed up a little; but during the long laboured climb to the crests it slowed almost to a stop, brooded over by a cloud of smoke that grew ever thicker and blacker. Yet strangely, in the end it was that very pall of smoke which saved them, blocking out the heat of the risen sun just long enough for the ship to limp into the shelter of the oasis.

'Mad it in the nickers team,' Walter sighed, and cut the engine, allowing the ship to coast to a halt.

The smoke cleared quickly, blown away by the mounting breeze, and in the sudden hush Anna understood why Walter had called this place Eden. After the barren beauty of the desert it was truly like a garden, a green and lovely retreat from the withering sunlight and arid reaches of the dunes. Here the air was cool, the ground shaded by tall palms that clustered thickly about a series of pools. Vines and other exotic growth clung to the trees; while at ground level the sandy soil was carpeted with an assortment of flowering plants. And through it all there blew a cool wind that rippled the surface of the pools and rustled the palm fronds.

'What a place!' Joe exclaimed. 'It's like ... like paradise.'

'No such location,' Trog commented, emerging from the rear cabin and punching the control button for the outer door. 'Paradise exists in realms of fantasy. Present site suitable for routine repairs. Temporary stay only.'

'Just passing through,' Og agreed.

'What a couple of unromantic souls,' Anna said with a laugh and led the way out of the ship. 'Let's leave them to it.'

Together, she and Joe walked slowly around the nearest pool and into the depths of the oasis, amazed at the riot of growth and colour that surrounded them. There had been nothing like this on Titan, with its harsh volcanic landscape; and even the pictures and holograms they'd been shown of Earth had not prepared them for this experience. Soon, with the ship blocked from view, it was as if they had stepped back in time and rediscovered a place of childhood dreams.

Anna paused in a sun-streaked clearing. 'I can hardly believe it,' she began, and stopped as it occurred to her that something was missing here. She looked around uneasily. What could it be? What exactly had she missed? There was nothing particularly out of . . .

Nothing! That one word was the key. For apart from the plants, almost nothing lived or moved. The trees and vines were empty. The ripe dates, which she and Joe had been picking up from the ground and eating, were too abundant, as though untouched until their arrival.

She looked at the date in her hand and quickly dropped it, fearing it might be poisoned.

'Anything the matter?' Joe asked.

She turned towards him. 'Haven't you noticed? There are no birds.'

He nodded. 'You're right. Come to think of it I haven't spotted any other animals. What do you think's going on?'

'I can't work it out, but I don't think we should eat any more of the dates, just in case.'

He sniffed at the one he'd been eating. 'It smells all right.'

'What else could be wrong, then?'

He shrugged. 'We could be too far out in the desert. Maybe it's hard even for birds to get here.'

That didn't seem particularly likely; but then, as Anna had to admit, they were newcomers to Earth and were hardly in a position to judge such things. Certainly there was nothing threatening about the oasis. On the contrary, it continued as beautiful and peaceful as ever, a refuge from the mounting heat of the desert. Especially now, with the pools glittering in the sunlight.

'Yes, you could be right,' she said, kneeling beside the nearest pool. 'Being out of range of most animals would explain why it's so unspoiled.'

'Well, it's not going to stay unspoiled for much longer,' Joe warned her with a grin, and began stripping off his clothes. 'Come on. We may not have another chance to swim for ages.' Without waiting for her, he splashed out through the shallows and plunged into the blue-green depths.

She watched him knife down through the water, wanting to follow, but hesitant. Should she perhaps remain as lookout – though for what? Surely the absence of other animals only made the place safer.

Half convinced, she was unbuttoning her shirt when several wisps of what she took to be palm fronds spiralled down and settled on the surface of the pool. She might have ignored them had they not immediately begun to sink, twisting sinuously as they headed for the bottom.

Palm fronds *sink*?

With a shudder she recognised them then, and shouted at the top of her lungs just as Joe came up for air. 'Snakes! There in the water! All round you!'

'Where?' He trod water for a moment before spotting them, and instantly began floundering towards the bank, with Anna urging him on.

On every side now she was aware of furtive movement, of long bodies gliding through the surrounding foliage – some almost finger-thin, others thicker than an arm. Their colouring was equally various, ranging from dull brown to brightest green and on to a dazzling display of stripes and spangles.

'Hurry!' she yelled. 'Hurry!' Snatching for his hand and yanking him free of the water; the two of them

81

abandoning his clothes and racing off between the trees.

All about them snake bodies were thumping onto the ground, some landing underfoot and making them dance aside. Yet somehow, through it all, they avoided the lunging heads and gaping mouths, their frantic dash carrying them clear.

From up ahead came the sound of the ship's alarm. So! The snakes were there too. Anna was convinced of it even before she spied the ship itself through a screen of vines. Trog and Og were stationed at the entrance ramp, plucking snakes from the grass and hurling them into the encircling trees. Yet there were too many to keep out, one lean shape of bronze and gold worming its way between Trog's legs and disappearing into the ship.

Anna and Joe reached the ramp only seconds later, leaping over the remaining snakes and half falling through the entrance.

Once inside they were immediately on their guard, checking out the shadowy corners of the cabin. Drawing a blank, they had just begun a search of the aft section when Walter's startled voice croaked a warning.

'Read a lot ... alert! I'm bor-bor-born dead ... bordered ... boarded!'

They spun around, their eyes settling on the air-conditioning vents. Could the snake have forced its way through one of the grilled openings?

'S-s-s-sneaks ... snacks ... snakes alive!' Walter shrieked, confirming their suspicions.

Joe ran to the nearest grille. 'We have to get that thing out of there!' he shouted, and turned to Trog and Og who were busy sealing the door.

'No device on board for penetrating inner workings of ship,' Trog announced dispassionately. 'Our task limited to securing cabins. That mission now accomplished. Reptiles unable to scale ship's smooth outer hull.'

'Snug as a bug in a rug,' Og put in chirpily.

'But there's a snake in amongst Walter's circuits!' Joe insisted.

'I repeat,' Trog droned. 'No device on board small enough to penetrate . . .'

He was interrupted by a squawk from Walter. 'Bear wear . . . beware the slide . . . slime . . . sly and su-su-subtle sermon . . . seapit . . . serpent!' he whispered, and with a burst of sparks the entrance lock slid open.

Trog made a grab for it, a blue shimmer of electrical charge darting along the surface of his limbs and making his whole body tremble; but he held on long enough to refasten the door.

'All s-s-secure,' he reported shakily, sounding more like Walter than his normal self.

'Oh the guide . . . the guise . . . the g-g-guile of it!' Walter complained bitterly. 'The keel . . . wheel . . . heel-bruising dafti . . . craftiness of this wor-wor-worm.' Then, in a strangely thoughtful voice, as if he were describing some momentous encounter: 'A snack cum to my watery tub/ On a hot-pot day, and I in my py-py-pyjies for the treat . . . heat,/ To wink . . . think . . . drink there.'

'Wait a minute, that's poetry!' Anna burst out, recognising the words. 'I've heard it before. It's from a fairly well-known poem.'

'So what?' Joe replied. 'How's that supposed to help us now?'

As if to illustrate his point, the engine rumbled into life; and it was only the fact that Trog had already disengaged the drive belts which prevented the ship from surging into the nearest pool.

'This is getting out of hand!' Joe said desperately as an upper locker sprang open, showering them with sealed canisters of food. 'We have to do something before . . .'

He stopped short as a body landed softly on the awning above their heads. He and Anna both looked up, expecting to see the curved outline of a snake; yet what crept to the awning's edge and peered down at them was a cat. Judging by its battered appearance it was one of the last of its kind there in the oasis . . . its tabby face badly scarred around the eyes and nose, one ear all but bitten off, its emaciated body ending with the limp and broken remnants of a tail.

'Where the hell did that come from?' Anna asked.

'Once domesticated order of felines,' Trog informed them, unperturbed as ever, 'noted for their agility.'

And Og, always more down to earth: 'Someone let the cat out of the bag.'

'I can see that,' Anna said as the battered animal leaped down and scurried over to the nearest corner.

It was plainly wary of them, flattening its one good ear and hissing for them to keep back; but just as plainly it was more frightened still of the snakes and had chosen this refuge in preference to life on the outside.

'Get the damned thing out of here!' Joe demanded, and Trog would have made a grab for it had Anna not intervened.

'No, hang on,' she said. 'I've got an idea.'

A sudden groan from Walter, followed by a hoarse reminder for them all to 'Be war!', only strengthened her resolve. Snatching up one of the food canisters, she broke it open, pulled out a morsel of preserved food, and offered it to the frightened animal. It hesitated and then, driven by hunger, took it from her with extraordinary delicacy, gulping it down and looking for more. She selected another scrap, but didn't feed it directly to the cat. Instead, she ordered Og to remove the nearest grille and tossed the scrap into the small rectangular opening.

The cat leaped in after it and immediately sensed the presence of the snake, for it gave a tigerish growl. Here, it seemed to be saying, was a single enemy that it could cope with; a lone creature like itself, as against the writhing mass of bodies that had attacked the ship. And with a further growl it crept off into the labyrinth of tunnels that honeycombed the space between wall and hull.

Walter's response was to let out an even louder squawk. 'Read a lot, murk two!' he screeched. 'Invent-vent-vador in my ...' The rest was cut off by a series of muffled thumps, each accompanied by the crackle of shorting circuits. Lights blew, lockers rattled open, sparks cascaded from electrical fittings, and on two separate occasions Trog again had to wrestle with the outer door.

Then, as abruptly as it had begun, it was over. One final thud, and after that only a soft rustle of movement along the lower wall.

They all waited, and with a sigh of relief saw the cat's face appear in the opening. Again it growled, but in triumph now, and stepped out into the cabin, dragging the dead body of the snake behind it.

'Hey! Not bad!' Joe said admiringly, and reached down to pat the cat's scarred head ... only to jerk back as the animal swiped at him.

With Anna it was far more friendly, laying the

snake at her feet as a gift, and accepting food straight from her hand.

'What shall we call you?' she crooned, while Joe discreetly disposed of the snake's body.

'Domestic felines indifferent to names,' Trog informed her.

While from Og: 'How about Puss in Boots?'

'Yes, Boots, that's who you'll be,' she said with a laugh, ruffling the soft fur beneath the cat's chin. 'For booting out an unwanted visitor.'

But it was Walter who paid his rescuer the highest tribute, by again reciting a jumbled version of a well-known poem. 'Trigger, Tigger, purring right,' he began in a croaky voice, 'In the freest of the night. What a muddle ... CLICK ... Water mortal ... CLICK ... What im-im-immortal hand or ... or ...'

He broke down completely at that point, retreating into silence, and for the rest of that day no amount of pleading from Anna or Joe could get another word from him. Though on this occasion they were less worried, aware that after any damaging experience he needed time to reorganise his circuits – or, as Anna secretly preferred to think, to heal himself.

Sure enough, at the onset of dusk he crackled back to life.

'Not a please aunt ex-ex-experience,' he announced, his voice surprisingly loud in the hush of evening, causing Boots to leap from Anna's lap and take refuge under the sleeping-capsule.

'D'you mean with the snake?' Joe asked.

He refused to answer directly. 'The pest of braces ... places and the wormiest of places,' he muttered. 'No one toll me that. Pilgrim ... pogrom ... program toll me, All career ... clear, no

86

buddy here. Not this natter-chatter, this tearful ... earful of worms and words.'

'What are you talking about, Walter?' Anna asked, crouching beside the now replaced grille.

'Stalk ... talking,' he repeated, and broke into a welcome gurgle of laughter. 'Yes, thus what I ear. Dud nut not-not-notice be fawn. Lotto noises ... voi-voi-voices. Lotto them.'

'Voices?' she took him up, curious. 'What kind of voices?'

'All salts,' he responded. 'All stalking to gather. List-list-listen.'

She cocked her head towards the open roof of the ship. And yes! She could hear something. But when she climbed up and peered out beneath the awning, all she saw was a flock of birds far to the south. They were making their way home across the desert, their distant cries just reaching her through the falling dusk.

'It's only birds, Walter,' she told him. 'That's all you can hear.'

'Gnome,' he disagreed. 'Lots of udders. So money of them.'

He would say nothing more after that, closing down for further readjustments.

'He's a worry, isn't he?' Joe whispered confidingly. 'I can't help wondering how close to the transports he'll manage to get us.'

Anna agreed. Though for her there was a further concern, one she couldn't quite put her finger on, which tied in with her lingering worry about the true nature of this Earth they had come to. Walter had spoken of voices, lots of them. What was that supposed to mean? Was he simply confused or was there really someone out there? Was it those same voices, perhaps, which were causing the snakes and all the other animals to act so peculiarly?

Baffled, she said nothing to Joe, preferring to push such troubled thoughts to the back of her mind, for the time being anyway. Yet later that evening, on the verge of sleep, she remembered the poem Walter had recited earlier, about the snake. She had been made to learn it, and now, in the eerie silence of the oasis, fragments of the closing lines came back to her: something about the snake being a 'king' and 'one of the lords of life'. A lord of life? Surely Walter didn't believe in such things. Surely! And if he did, then why describe a snake in that way?

But it had been a long and testing day. And secure in the knowledge that Trog and Og were standing guard, she snuggled closer to Joe and drifted off to sleep.

8

The snakes continued to swarm around the ship throughout the next day, making work on the damaged engine doubly difficult. As Walter had pointed out soon after landing, neither Trog nor Og was designed for such a delicate task; and with one of them having to stand watch at all times, the work went on for hour after hour. As a result it was evening before the engine was more or less serviceable.

'This is one place I won't be sorry to leave,' Joe declared, gazing out over the deceptive beauty of the oasis.

Boots clearly felt the same. Already at ease in his new home, he was parading around the upper edge of the hull, his battered tail held rakishly aloft, a look of disdain on his face as he surveyed the snakes below.

Only Anna had mixed feelings about leaving. She was frightened of the oasis, it was true, but also intrigued by it, suspecting that the key to Earth's mysteries lay as much here as anywhere. On the other hand, as Joe had been pointing out all day, their primary duty was to reach the transports and activate the incubators. Until they had actually started the new colony, nothing else mattered. It was what they were there for.

On that score at least Anna couldn't help but agree. So when Walter broke his silence to announce that they should 'Stan boy for the pasture,' she laughed as heartily as Joe, though not perhaps with quite as much relief.

'Engine ready to activate,' Trog warned them, and it hummed into life.

'Let's hit the road,' Og added, and with a noisy rumble the ship nosed between two stands of palms and slid out into the desert.

Within minutes it was as if the previous two days had hardly existed. The great waves of the desert rolled on as before; the splendour of the Milky Way arched above them like some endless highway they had never left; and with the coming of full night Walter resumed his song.

'Someone's happy to be on the move again,' Joe observed.

'If your stalking bout jaws truly,' Walter responded, without breaking off his song, 'then your bright. Nutting like a starry barry light to make you hoppy.'

'Why's that, Walter?' Joe asked, trying not to laugh.

'I toll you. It rewinds me of the race ... grace ... face of good.'

Anna saw the opening and couldn't resist it. 'Does that have a voice too, Walter?'

There was a brief pause, with the ship rumbling away beneath them and the night wind blowing cool on their cheeks.

'Herd to say,' he replied at last, an odd caginess in his tone. 'Too money voi-voi-voices to tell.'

'How many?' she pressed him.

'Like ... like ...' He seemed to be groping for

words that were beyond him. 'Like cranes of sand on the bush.'

'On the beach, d'you mean?'

'Yes, on the bush ... bash ... b-b-beach. Money as fat ... as that.'

'That's a lot, Walter,' she said carefully, as though agreeing with him. 'You've really got me wondering about these voices. Are you sure they're not coming from ... well, from inside you?'

'Yeah, maybe they're echoes from your abandoned circuits,' Joe suggested, and was greeted by a boyish chuckle.

'Don't be filly,' Walter said. 'I'm not g-g-good.'

'We didn't say you were,' Anna pointed out.

'Neither did I,' Walter came back to her, and with an audible 'click' he withdrew, leaving behind only his wordless song.

'Well, that didn't get us anywhere,' Joe observed in a whisper. 'If you ask me he doesn't know what he's talking about half the time. As for hearing voices! We all know what that means, don't we?'

Anna pondered the idea as the ship ploughed on through the dark. On the face of it Joe was right: under the stress of the journey Walter was going quietly insane. Or so it seemed. Yet somehow she felt uneasy with that explanation. Walter's caginess, plus his bewildering talk of countless voices, suggested something else; that maybe he had begun to understand certain things about this planet; that he had gained some secret knowledge back there at the oasis. But knowledge of what?

She sifted rapidly through the various things he had told them over the past two days. 'This is the best of places and the worst of places,' he had said at one stage. Now what was that supposed to mean?

And only ten minutes ago: 'I'm not God.'

No, wait a minute. She brought herself up short. What he had *actually* said was, 'I'm not good.' So which was it? God or good? And either way, how did that fit in with all his talk of voices?

As baffled as ever, she gave up the struggle and turned her attention to the surrounding night. Joe was already asleep, slumped in the seat beside her. His face, honest and open – not stupid, but not particularly clever either – served to remind her how different he was from Walter. Well, that was something to be thankful for. Though for the moment she was glad to be free of them both. To be alone for a change. Or at least as alone as Boots would allow, his warm body curled up contentedly on her lap.

Now *there's* a kind of wisdom, she decided with a smile, stroking his scarred head. So why not think like a cat? And she made an effort to relax, emptying her mind and allowing the night to flow into her.

The effect was satisfying. For a while she lost track of time, living only through her immediate senses. Directly ahead, starlight glittered on the crests of the dunes; all around her Walter's song rose and fell, keeping time to the sigh of the wind; and with the paddlewheel grumbling away in the background she also succumbed to sleep.

Or more exactly, to a dream in which Boots spoke to her in one of the secret voices which, until then, only Walter had been able to hear. 'You see what I mean,' Walter murmured slyly from the sidelines. But it was Boots she was interested in, not him. With his one good ear cocked and alert, he was telling her things she dearly wanted to know. The trouble was, although the words themselves made perfect sense, she couldn't hold onto them. Their meaning kept slipping away like sand through her fingers. Slow down, she tried telling him, but her own mouth proved strangely voiceless. And soon even Boots' words were drowned out by a boom and crash so loud that she jerked awake and gazed out into the grey of dawn.

To her surprise the booming noise went on.

'Are we breaking down again?' she muttered thickly, struggling to sit up.

'All systems in order,' Trog replied promptly.

And Og, as he handed her a morning drink: 'We're fit as a fiddle.'

She realised then that the ship had stopped and the noise was coming from elsewhere. Also, someone had opened the outer door and Joe and Boots had disappeared.

'Where are we, Walter?' she demanded, peering through the windscreen which for some reason was blurry with moisture.

'At the moat ... mate ... meeting pace of the voi-voi-voices,' he answered.

'Try again,' she said irritably. 'In plain English this time.'

'Ahem.' He pretended to clear his throat. 'Two salts of voi-voi-voices spiking here. One form the band ... strand ... land. Udder form the want ... wart ... water.'

'Water?' she took him up, fully awake now, and made for the door.

She emerged onto a windswept beach piled high with silvered driftwood. It was backed by a last line of dunes, a cliff edge of sand that had collapsed in places, undercut by the crash and surge of the breakers. Through one of these gaps the ship had made its way, gliding to within a dozen paces of the surf.

And what a surf! What a sea! For Anna, reared on the uneventful plains of Titan, it was like coming face to face with a thing both monstrous and beautiful. Nothing had prepared her for it, not even the holograms she had studied just before their departure. This was immense! Terrifying! A blue-grey vista of water which seemed to march relentlessly towards her. Only the steepness of the beach prevented it flooding inland, the heave and crash of each wave making her cower against the ship's hull.

'What do you think?' someone shouted through the uproar.

She turned and saw Joe grinning at her, his eyes alive with excitement. Boots, distinctly less happy, sat hunched on Joe's shoulder, his coat gleaming from the spray.

'Do we have to cross *that*?' she shouted back.

Joe's grin faltered slightly, but stayed bravely in place. 'So Walter says. Though he hasn't explained how.'

'Well, let's hope he knows what he's doing,' she said, trying to match Joe's tone, and with a last nervous glance at the incoming breakers she retreated to the safety of the cabin.

There the transformers were already hard at work, stripping away the upper section of the interior wall and revealing Walter's inner workings.

'So what's the plan, Walter?' Joe asked suspiciously.

'Rolly Dodger time,' was the reply.

'What sort of time?'

'Time for the J-j-jolly Roger.'

Joe continued to stare blankly at the rapid dismantling of the cabin wall, but already a dark suspicion had entered Anna's mind.

94

'When pirates were around there were only sailing ships,' she reminded Walter. 'They depended just on the wind.'

'My pont ... port ... point ex-ex-exactly,' he responded.

'You mean you intend *sailing* across that sea out there?'

But at that moment Trog began transferring the exposed circuits to the lower wall cavity, and Walter's answer came out hopelessly garbled.

'Water rung with soiling the Russians Blue? Agest spot gnome to man kindle. Where yawn spearmint of ...?'

The rest was lost in the general din as Trog and Og set about removing the unwanted insulation and cutting away the upper section of the hull. One by one the severed metal sheets slid onto the sand, until soon the wind was blowing fiercely through the exposed cabin. To escape it, Anna and Joe had to duck below what was left of the outer wall, which now stood little more than a metre high.

'He's turning the damned thing into an open boat!' Joe grated out, powerless to stop the two transformers who went about their work with almost deadly intent. 'How does he expect us to cross an ocean in this? He should take a look at those seas out there.'

'Look dully taken,' Walter informed them unexpectedly. 'Truss me.'

He fell silent again as the transformers scurried outside and began removing both engines.

'Now what?' Anna said, watching helplessly as Og, staggering under the weight, supported each of the engines in turn while Trog bolted and welded them to the sides of the ship like giant outriggers.

By then she and Joe had retreated to the shelter of

a heap of driftwood further up the beach. Boots, in a high state of alarm, had wedged himself between them, his skinny body quivering in response to each fresh outbreak of noise from the ship.

'Can't Walter see that the weight of those two engines will drag the hull down?' Joe broke out in exasperation.

But he was soon shown to be wrong, for during the next hour Trog welded metal plates to the intakes and exhausts of both engines, sealing off their combustion chambers and turning them into buoyancy tanks. With one on either side of the ship there was little chance of its sinking. To give the craft added stability, a shallow keel was then fashioned from what remained of the metal stripped from the upper part of the hull – with Trog and Og hammering away until it was as sleek and smooth as a shark's fin.

Darkness fell long before they could attach it to the underside of the ship. And Anna and Joe, rather than return to the exposed cabin where they would only have felt in the way, scooped out a shallow cave beneath the driftwood and took shelter there.

With some help from Og they soon had a fire burning in the cave mouth, and after that they felt reasonably snug. The activity at the ship, like the constant booming of the waves, continued somewhere off in the darkness, but for the present they ignored it, content with their own small circle of warmth and light.

'This is how people must have lived thousands of years ago,' Anna observed dreamily, gazing up past the fireglow to the wide sweep of the stars.

They had long since cooked and eaten a simple meal and were sprawled on the sand, the security of the cave at their backs.

'There're still big differences between us and them,' Joe reminded her. 'In the past, people had to share Earth with large and dangerous animals. Life's a lot safer here now.'

'I didn't feel too safe when the ship was surrounded by snakes,' she pointed out. 'Or up there on the mountain being attacked by rats.'

He nodded vaguely, as if only half agreeing with her. 'Yeah, I know what you mean, but imagine what it was like when bears and lions and wolves were roaming around out there. That would have been much worse.'

Would it? she wondered, and remembered with a shudder the way the rat had plopped down on her face. At the time it had seemed the worst possible thing that could happen to her. During those few agonising seconds she would gladly have traded the squirming body of the rat for a charging lion or even a pack of wolves. Then too there had been that weird look in the rat's eyes, a look she still found unnerving. Or was she just being silly? A rat, after all, was a puny thing compared with a bear or a lion. The birds' attack on the rat nest had proved that.

'Yes, I suppose Earth is a lot safer than it was,' she agreed reluctantly.

But the words were hardly out of her mouth when a yowling cry issued from the dark, bringing them both scrambling to their feet. There was a swish and flurry somewhere off in the gloom, and Boots suddenly appeared, running at full tilt. Racing past them, he dived into the cave and flattened himself against the rear wall.

'Well, something put the fear of death into him,' Joe observed shakily.

That 'something' showed itself briefly as a series of flitting shadows, impossible to identify. There was a glint of eyes at the far limits of the firelight, and then they were gone.

Boots seemed to sense straight away that he was safe because his fur lost its bristly look and he padded up to Anna and began rubbing the side of his face against her arm. Even so, they were more careful after that, building up the fire and crawling into the cave to sleep.

Anna woke twice in the course of the night. The first time she barely surfaced, half roused by the crackling of the fire as Joe heaped it with fresh wood. On the second occasion she came more fully awake. Joe was breathing evenly beside her and the night was inky black, the fire having burned down to a dull bank of coals. Careful not to disturb Joe, she crawled from the cave and was groping for a stick of wood when she saw the eyes again. Much closer than before, a whole row of them now, watching her from the dark. Whatever the creatures were, they made no sound, not even when she threw the stick at them. The eyes merely blinked out for a few moments and reappeared – a little nearer, she noted with a shiver.

She didn't try attacking them again, but busied herself with the fire – blowing the coals into life and then patiently feeding the flames. Not until she had built up a good blaze did she crawl back beside Joe and give herself to sleep.

The sun was up, the air misty with spray, when next she woke. Joe was bending over her with a plate of food and a hot drink.

'Wait till you see what they've made of the ship,' he said ominously.

She tried to scramble past him, but he pushed her back.

'No, eat first,' he advised her. 'You'd better be prepared for this.'

The food, cooked over the open fire, had a tangy, smoky flavour, as did the drink; and she was feeling pleasantly full and ready for just about anything when she emerged onto the windswept beach.

The ship, as Joe had warned her, was completely transformed. Mounted on logs for easy launching, and with its twin outriggers and keel attached, it had become a low-slung open boat. Gone was the upper swell of its body, the hull cut off a little below the level of the windscreen, which had been left in place as a partial protection against wind and wave. Gone, too, were its supporting struts and runners. These had been refashioned into two stumpy masts, one mounted in the main cabin, the other further astern, near the tail-like rudder; and each of these masts sported a triangular sail made from the awning and the extra strip of insulation taken from the hull. Both sails now fluttered and cracked in the wind as though urging Anna and Joe to hurry aboard.

'Do you think it's seaworthy?' Anna asked, glancing nervously from the boat to the line of incoming waves.

'I suppose there's only one way to find out,' Joe answered, and led the way across the beach.

'Red eye to go?' Walter greeted them cheerily. 'Climb a bird.'

'How do you propose we do that?' Joe challenged him, for the remains of the door had been welded closed.

A knotted rope came snaking over the side.

'Make hast, my hurt ... heat ... hearties,' Walter

sang out in what remained of his pirate voice. 'The toad ... tyre ... tide is on the torn.'

Joe grasped the rope, but still hesitated. 'Are you sure we can survive in this thing?'

'Shore?' Walter laughed. 'Nutting shore in this wickered weld.'

'You know what Joe means,' Anna cut in. 'Can we really stay afloat in heavy seas?'

'Heaven sees?' he queried, and she suspected he was making fun of them now. 'Jesus ... jest ... just truss old Wal-wal-wallie, like airways.'

So it was a question of trust again, Anna thought grimly as she handed Boots up to Og and clambered after Joe.

'Standby for lunch,' Walter sang out happily.

'Ready to roll,' Og echoed him.

From below there came a steady 'thock, thock' as Trog knocked aside the wedges holding the craft in position. He swarmed aboard as the ship surged forward on its launching pad of turning logs – he and Og rapidly securing the sails which snapped full, accelerating their progress down the beach. Trog just had time to reach the tiller before they rode up onto the wash of a spent wave, slewed slightly, and turned resolutely into the wind.

They were afloat! Exhilarated, Anna turned to meet the oncoming sea ... and immediately wished she had done anything but that, wished herself anywhere but where she was, directly in the path of the next towering wave. How impossibly tall it looked, looming above them. How coldly green and glassy, a thing without thought or feeling. And the noise of it! A steady roar that blotted out every other sound.

She couldn't move. Couldn't even think clearly. Yet still, in those few breathless seconds before it struck, she knew – *knew* in her innermost self – that they had made a mistake. That they should never have trusted their lives to the poor, flawed remains of someone like Walter.

Part 2
SONG OF THE SEA

9

Joe was about to follow Boots' example and dive for cover behind the windscreen when something prompted him to glance sideways, to where Anna, frozen with terror, was staring up at the looming wave.

'Anna!' he yelled above the roar of the surf, and tried to pull her down with him, but her body, made rigid by panic, refused to bend, her hand slipping from his as the wave swept over them.

Lost in a welter of water and foam, all he could do was grab for the nearest handhold and hang on, the craft shuddering beneath him. For a few moments he thought it would founder altogether, sucked down by the undertow. Then, with a shake, it wallowed clear, dragging him up into the light and air.

As he had feared, Anna was gone, and frantically he searched the surrounding surf, ready if need be to dive overboard.

'Anna!' he screamed, for the second time, and to his relief he was answered by a feeble shout.

He saw her then, more than halfway down the

deck. With her hair plastered across her face, she clung blindly to the shorter of the two masts. Behind her and chest deep in water, Og was busy wrestling with a wildly flapping sail that threatened to flog itself to shreds, while further back still, Trog heaved at the tiller, struggling to point the craft into the wind before the next wave struck.

'Hold on, I'm coming!' he shouted, and was floundering towards her when there was a roar from directly behind him. The deck tilted alarmingly, the rush of onboard water carrying him before it; and even as his clutching fingers locked around the forward mast, another wave crashed down.

He really believed they were gone that time, the whole craft shuddering as it fought its way through the underwater gloom. With a jolting impact the keel hit bottom and lodged in the sand long enough for the wave to pass. Then once again they wallowed free, a gust of wind snapping the sails full and driving them forward.

Despite the water they had taken on board they reached the next wave before it could break. Hissing viciously it passed beneath them, leaving them teetering in space, the foam from its crest speckling the air like snow. Slowly at first, and then with a sickening rush, they plunged into the waiting trough and buried their nose in the oncoming sea. But again their straining sails pushed them on and up, the crest flicking past and crashing down astern.

Wave after wave followed, each less threatening than the one before. And Joe, no longer in danger of being swept overboard, succeeded at last in moving over to where Anna still clung to the mast.

'Walter did it!' she burst out, laughing up at him as he wound both arms about her. 'He did it!'

It was on the tip of Joe's tongue to say that Trog and Og were the ones who had seen them through, but he said nothing, not wanting to question her faith in Walter. Especially now, with the shoreline right there at their back and the boat still low in the water.

'Come on,' he murmured, and they struggled forward, to where Boots, wet and bedraggled and looking very sorry for himself, sat shivering on the ledge beneath the windscreen.

The deck was draining rapidly now, water pouring out through vents in the stern; and as the boat rose higher they picked up speed, the sails tugging them clear of the coastal shelf. Soon the breakers were no more than a line of foam in the distance – a cotton wool fringe to the grey-brown bulge of the land – and they were skimming easily over the long blue swells of the open sea.

'I can report that ship has suffered no serious damage,' Trog intoned from his place at the tiller. 'Loss of only peripheral circuits. All basic functions intact.'

And Og, as unaffected by their recent soaking as his companion: 'Happy to say we're right as rain.'

As if prompted by them, Walter also stirred into life. There was a spluttering noise followed by a dribble of water from the air-conditioning ducts, and then: 'This plank ... plant ... planet can be a rule tri-tri-trial sun times.'

So can you, Joe was tempted to say, but again he held back.

He was glad he had, for Anna was clearly delighted with Walter's performance. 'I think we can survive anything after that,' she said, running her hand affectionately along the inner wall. 'You were marvellous, Walter.'

'Degreed,' he answered smugly. 'We neatly come unsuck . . . stork . . . stuck there. Never mine. As Og would stay, "All swill that end swill".' And with a crow of youthful laughter he began singing his version of 'Life on the Ocean Way'.

Within minutes, however, he had grown more serious, the old-fashioned song giving place to his usual wordless melody, which seemed to drift up and down with the great swells that stretched away to the horizon. Even Joe had to admit it was a soothing sound, and comforted by it he set about helping Anna and Og to clear the last remnants of water from the decks and check the ship's compartments. In most of them, fortunately, the seals had held, so there was little loss of food or equipment. More important still, there was not so much as a hint of damp in the sleeping-capsule. The one real disappointment was that all the video-screens had shorted out, which meant that Walter had no way of showing them maps of what lay ahead.

'Not that it matters all that much,' Anne observed trustingly. 'Walter knows what he's doing.'

Joe dearly wished he could share her confidence, but the fact was he couldn't . . . and it was more than just Walter's garbled speech that concerned him. The problem went deeper than that. Joe's underlying worry was the irrational element that had crept into Walter's behaviour. The highly logical personality they had set out with had deteriorated first into a playful child and then into some sort of madman who sang to himself for hours on end and claimed he could hear voices.

Nor was that Joe's only concern. He was also worried about Anna, his fondness for her and his worry all tangled together in a way he found hard to understand. Back on Titan she had been so steady, so practical, but after the landing she had changed. The turning point had been the attack by those rats. It must have unsettled her badly because she'd been far more fanciful ever since.

Take for example her theory about some super intelligence controlling all the animals on Earth. As far as Joe was concerned it just didn't add up. For one thing there was no real evidence of any outside agency. For another, Anna's theory assumed that the animals themselves had stayed more or less the same over recent centuries – whereas it stood to reason that once people abandoned the planet, everything had started to evolve again. With the dominant species gone, the other animals had been free to change, to organise themselves, to develop in wholly new directions. By learning to live and hunt together, to co-operate, they had merely filled the vacuum left by humans. Why, in time they might even . . .

But his train of thought was interrupted by Og. 'Time to feed the inner man,' he announced, handing Joe a pannikin of hot food.

Trog offered Anna a similar container with the more sober observation: 'Requisite midday sustenance.'

Midday already! Surprised at how quickly the hours had slipped by, Joe looked about him. The eastern shore had disappeared altogether. They were surrounded now by nothing but ocean, the horizon unbroken in every direction. The seas remained quite high, the wind blowing keenly across their quarter and bellying out the sails, but the swells were much longer out here, the craft riding them in a slow rocking motion.

'I wouldn't mind knowing where we're headed,' Joe remarked once they had finished eating.

Anna shrugged indifferently, her eyes following the progress of a giant seabird cruising in their wake. 'We're in safe hands with Walter.'

'I'd like to know all the same,' he insisted, and rapped with his knuckles on the windscreen. 'Walter, can you give us an update?'

The song faltered and there was a kind of sigh, as if Joe's request were an unwanted distraction. 'Immod ... Immac ... immediate dusty nation is large land mess lick ... luck ... located due best ... west.'

'Is that where the transports landed?'

'Connect. In typical ... topical ... tropical relig ... region cluster shore.'

'How close to the shore?' Joe pressed him.

He sighed again. 'Work ... welk ... walking distance,' he answered shortly.

'So once we land we can leave you and go on ahead with the transformers?'

'Connect,' he repeated, and resumed his song, discouraging further discussion.

'Not exactly communicative, is he?' Joe complained.

'I expect he has a lot on his mind,' Anna answered absently, and pointed to the bird still hovering in their wake. 'I've been watching that bird. It's had its eye on us for an hour or more now.'

Joe gazed up at it, noting its huge wingspan and the ease with which it rode the wind. 'I think it's called an albatross. They're well known for following ships.'

'It seems to be doing more than that,' she said thoughtfully. 'You should see the look in its eyes when it comes close. You'd swear it's trying to work out what we're doing here.'

'You can tell that just from its eyes?'

'Okay, maybe that's a bit far fetched,' she conceded. 'All the same, birds aren't supposed to look at you that way. This one makes me feel it's . . . it's *monitoring* us; that something else is looking through its eyes.'

'You mean we're being spied on?'

She must have heard the alarm in his voice because she gave him a reassuring smile and reached for his hand.

'No, not exactly. I'm just trying to explain my feelings about this place, that's all.'

He returned the pressure of her hand. 'D'you know what I think?' he said carefully. 'I reckon we've been through too much over the past few days. We're not seeing things clearly any more. That's why we shouldn't jump to conclusions. We should keep open minds, at least until we reach the transports.'

'What if we don't reach them?' she asked quietly. 'Have you considered that?'

He nodded, deciding to be honest with her. 'Last night when I got up to tend the fire, there were eyes watching us from the dark, lots of them, and I felt scared in spite of the fire. I wondered then whether we'd ever make it to the rendezvous.'

She sidled closer. 'I saw the eyes too. Did they make you wish you'd never left Titan? It may not have been a beautiful place, with its bare lava plains and endless rain. Not beautiful like Earth anyway. But it was safe.'

He didn't answer straight away, brooding on the blue-black waves which rose like hillocks on every side.

111

'I can't say I really regret coming here,' he said at last. 'What Walter said about us is probably true. We're nothing special. We were only chosen as the first parents *because* we're ordinary and dependable. Well, I don't care about that any more. What matters is that we've been rescued from a boring existence on Titan. Just think about it: we could have spent the whole of our lives there, on a planet where human beings are the only major life-form; where there are no plants and trees, and all the food has to be grown in breeder tanks. No, this was our one chance of adventure, and we'd be fools to regret it. That's why we shouldn't panic about this place,' he added meaningfully. 'If we start getting wrong ideas about it, we could wreck the one big chance we'll ever have.'

He paused, hoping his veiled appeal would strike home, but again she seemed distracted.

'Take a look at Boots,' she murmured. 'What do you think he's up to?'

He turned to where Boots was staring at his own reflection in the windscreen.

'He's not up to anything that I can see. He's just curious. That's how cats are supposed to be.'

'Curiosity killed the cat,' Og chanted obligingly.

'But he hasn't moved for ten minutes or more,' Anna pointed out. 'Surely it's not normal for a cat to concentrate *that* long.'

'What about when they're hunting.'

'Yes, but he isn't hunting, is he? He's just sitting there gazing at himself.'

'So what do *you* think it means?'

'I've told you,' she whispered, and drew him further away as though worried that Boots might overhear. 'Something funny's going on. No ordinary cat would act like that. There has to be a reason for it.'

'Listen, Anna,' he said impatiently. 'We've been through all this before and I don't see things your way. Cats are like all the other species we've come across so far: they've probably changed over the centuries. They act differently now. There's no big mystery hidden behind everything.'

But before the argument could go any further they were interrupted by Walter.

'Voi-voi-voices from the weep ... beep ... deep!' he screeched, his song cutting out altogether.

'Voices?' Anna swung around so abruptly that Boots gave a nervous mew and dived for cover. 'Are you sure?'

'Shorn as I'm flute ... flight ... floating year.'

'What are they saying?'

'Not spiking in whorls ... worms ... words. All mirages are clouded ... Correction: All mess-mess-messages are coded.'

'What do they sound like then?'

'List-list-listen,' Walter instructed them, and a series of clicks and beeps filled the air.

'How do you know that's a code?' Joe objected. 'It could be radio static, anything.'

'Most codes show evidence of underlying pattern,' Trog explained from his post at the tiller. 'Non-manufactured sounds are more random.'

And Og, refusing as usual to be left out: 'There are no whispers in the wind, no babblings in the brooks.'

'If those really are coded messages,' Joe added, 'you should be able to crack them easily enough. What are they on about?'

'Too curly to till,' Walter responded. 'Compo ...

113

computing power lim-lim-limited. Circuses over ludo ... laden. Time needled to dec-decipher the sarong of the seal.'

'The what?' Anna asked, puzzled.

Yet all at once it was Joe who was the one straining forward, listening for all he was worth, a chill breath of suspicion catching him unawares.

'The sing ... sung ... song of the sea,' Walter repeated, and promptly withdrew, his own song swelling out again.

'Any idea what he meant by that?' Anna queried.

'Haven't a clue,' Joe lied, and turned away so she wouldn't see his face.

The song of the sea! Could that really be the answer to Anna's mystery? he asked himself, groping past his earlier doubt towards an altogether unexpected solution. Had they finally stumbled on the truth out there in the middle of the ocean? No. He shook his head imperceptibly. It wasn't possible. Not after all this time. Yet still the suspicion persisted, his eyes drawn almost against his will towards the unrevealing surface of the sea.

10

'Walter's taking his time about deciphering those messages,' Joe complained, restlessly pacing the forward deck.

It was late afternoon, the sun peeping beneath a heavy bank of stormcloud far to the west. As it sank lower it created a glittering path of light on the surface of the sea, like an uneven road along which the ship toiled steadily. Already, in anticipation of the coming storm, much of that road was streaked with foam as the rising wind whipped the tops off the waves.

'He's probably struggling with a really hard code,' Anna suggested.

She and Boots sat crouched together in the capsule, its raised lid protecting them from the heavier gusts of wind.

'Or better still,' Joe added as a hopeful after-thought, 'maybe there's no code to be cracked. Maybe Walter just dreamed up the idea of hidden messages.'

'I doubt it,' Anna said. 'He may not be as bright as he was, but he's still far from dumb. He wouldn't waste time on a lot of random noises. There's something out here with us, the same as there was something following us on land. If we're lucky, this time

Walter will find out what it is. Personally I don't care if it takes him all night.'

All night? Joe stared impatiently at the westering sun. Having already begun to suspect the truth about this place – what he now thought of as its *ancient* truth – he was eager for it to be confirmed. The idea of waiting a whole night seemed intolerable. He wouldn't be able to sleep, he was sure of that, visualising the hours ahead as simply boring and uneventful.

Yet not for the first time he had reckoned without the intervention of the planet. Or at least of one of its more sinister inhabitants.

The first they knew of the coming crisis was when Trog sounded a warning from the stern. 'Alien presence in immediate vicinity,' he intoned.

Og for once had nothing to say, merely tightening the ropes attached to the sails as if readying the ship for changed conditions.

'What does he mean, an alien presence?' Joe began, and stopped as a shudder passed rapidly through the ship.

Anna pushed Boots aside and sprang up. 'What was that? Walter, are you with us?'

But Walter was too preoccupied with his 'voices' even to be roused.

The ship shuddered again, as if some giant body had rubbed itself along the keel, and Joe and Anna ran quickly to the rail. They were just in time to see a dark mass slide past beneath the surface.

'Was that a whale?' Joe asked, for the thing had been huge, longer than the ship and nearly as broad.

'We'll soon see,' Anna answered, scanning the surrounding waves. 'Whales are mammals like us; they have to come up for air.'

They both waited, on the lookout for a plume of spray; but minutes passed, the sun sinking lower, and only the wind disturbed the long, crested swells.

Had the creature perhaps circled back and come up on the other side? Joe was about to check when the ship shuddered yet again, more violently than before, rising out of the water and slewing around.

'Red alert. Ship under attack,' Trog announced in his usual unruffled manner, and brought them back on course.

'Batten down the hatches!' Og added, and hurried forward to close the capsule.

He had barely done so when the ship was struck with enough force to lift it clear of the oncoming wave. Joe and Anna, clinging desperately to the rail, glimpsed a great chisel head directly beneath them, followed by a huge dorsal fin. Then the whole ship lurched sideways and crashed back down, taking on board a rush of water before managing to right itself.

Knee-deep in the swirling water, Joe and Anna looked at each other in dismay.

'Shark!' Anna broke out hoarsely, confirming Joe's own worst fears.

But what a shark! He had had no idea they could get that big. The officials on Titan, who had prepared them for the trip, had insisted that most of the large animals had perished. Though of course it would have been different here in the sea, where deep-swimming creatures like sharks would have suffered less damage from dangerous levels of ultra-violet light. Yes, that explained it, Joe concluded hastily – and was knocked off his feet by another grinding blow, this one finally alerting Walter.

'Hell . . . hull taking wattle!' he cried. 'Circuses

fold ... fooled ... flooding. Clothing down to pres-pres-preserve ...' Before he could finish there was an ominous click, audible above the noise of the wind, and after that nothing.

'We're on our own!' Anna sang out, making a grab for Boots who was being washed from one side of the craft to the other.

'No, there's still Trog,' Joe shouted back, and floundered across to the rail.

The sun had almost reached the horizon. The approaching stormclouds loomed above it, giving to the evening an angry, brooding quality. A peal of thunder rolled across the ocean like a warning, and as the ship crested the next wave Joe was given his first clear view of the shark.

It was angling towards them, its dorsal fin slicing through the darkening water, its mouth so distended that its chisel-shaped nose kept breaking the surface.

'Ready to come about,' Trog called calmly, and swung the tiller with such force that the ship heeled sharply and lurched away to the south; and the shark, instead of colliding with the already damaged hull, crashed into the engine-cum-outrigger.

There was a splintering of teeth and a flurry of foam as the engine's hardened casing withstood the pressure of those jaws. Yet still the shark refused to release its hold. Using its body, it jerked its head furiously, shaking the craft from stem to stern and dragging it under so that water again poured in over the sides.

Only then did it back off, though not in order to retreat. As it wallowed alongside, one large round eye fully exposed, Joe could have sworn it was assessing the state of its prey. That watchful eye swivelled slightly and fixed itself on him, as if singling him out from the rest of the craft. Targeting him. Just for an instant, as the eye glinted knowingly, he had the distinct impression that the creature was telling him something. You, it seemed to be saying, I have chosen you! No one else. Then, before Joe could decide whether or not he was dreaming, the shark was driving forward.

'Get down!' Anna screamed.

And Trog, louder still, his calm voice carrying clear above the noise of wind and wave: 'Stand ready to jibe.'

Again he wrenched at the tiller; again the craft heeled over, one of the sails nearly tearing loose as it was punched across; and with a clubbing action the stern turned through the wind and struck the advancing shark.

It retaliated by slashing at the rudder, sending splinters of metal flying. Next it dived deep and savaged the keel, the whole craft shuddering under the impact.

'We can't take much more of this!' Anna shouted, clutching at Joe for support.

He drew her close, watching across her shoulder as the shark surfaced some distance ahead and prepared for its final run. In the day's dying light, with the sun's upper edge trembling on the horizon, he caught a last glint from those strangely watchful eyes and braced himself for what was to come.

Long before the shark could close in, however, several smaller shapes arced across its path. Dolphins! Others, golden in the fading light, curved and danced about it, while others again rose through the shadowy waters and formed a wedge of living bodies between shark and ship. Simultaneously an excited chorus of clicks and beeps was carried on the wind – sounds

119

which Joe immediately recognised as Walter's mysterious voices. Is that all they were? he thought, oddly disappointed. Just the cries of dolphins? Though for the present none of that mattered. The important thing was the way a small group of dolphins had peeled off from the rest. With high-pitched cries, inviting the ship to accompany them, they headed for the darkest patch of the horizon where a mass of stormcloud blotted out what little remained of the day. 'Come,' they seemed to be saying, 'Come,' some of them pausing in their flight to look back.

Joe glanced again at the shark which was thrashing this way and that in an attempt to break through the living cordon, and he made up his mind on the instant.

'Follow them!' he shouted, pointing towards the departing animals.

'Inadvisable,' Trog responded. 'Eye of storm in that direction.'

'Just do it!' Anna shouted in turn.

And with Trog's metal hand steady on the tiller, and Og trimming their one remaining sail, they turned and followed the now dusky bodies of the dolphins into the night.

Listing badly after the punishment it had taken, the ship could do little more than limp along, moving up the long swells with painful slowness. In sharp contrast, the storm advanced at astonishing speed, its thunder rolls drowning out the dolphins' ever more distant cries. Soon those cries had faded altogether, the animals fleeing into the dark as if conscious that their job was done. Thereafter the only sounds apart from the thunder were the rising howl of the wind and the crash of waves across the ship's labouring bows.

In a series of lightning flashes Joe glimpsed the towering seas ahead. Then, mercifully, they were blotted out as the rain hissed down, swamping the decks that had so recently been cleared.

'We'll freeze if we stay out in this,' Anna shouted, her mouth close to his ear, and she urged him over to the capsule.

Huddled inside, with Boots cowering between them, all they could do was look on as the damaged ship was buffeted by wind and wave. More than once they thought they would founder, but always the ship fought its way clear, shaking off the weight of water that streamed across its decks. And throughout it all both Trog and Og stood firm, nursing the damaged rudder and the one poor scrap of sail, their eyes glowing faintly red in the darkness.

It was those unblinking eyes that Joe searched for at the blackest of moments, their unwavering glow giving him new hope; and it was those same eyes, like beacons in the gloom of a far deeper night, that he dreamed of when, exhausted by the continual pummelling, he curled up beside Anna and fell asleep.

For a while the wind pursued him even there – a voice of madness, of unreason, that whispered cunningly around the edges of his dreams. On several occasions, unnerved by it, he started awake, but always he drifted back to sleep as someone – Anna? – reached through the dark and held him close.

He had no idea when the wind dropped. He opened his eyes and knew only that it was morning and at last the world was silent again. Anna was sitting up beside him, her face washed by sunlight that streamed in through the capsule's clear cover. She seemed to be gazing at something, a half smile playing about her lips.

'Look,' she said, sensing he was awake. 'Over there.'

He sat up and saw it – an island, not more than a kilometre or two away, rising almost vertically from the sea. A great rocky fortress of a place, it was topped by lush green forest, its sheer granite sides festooned with vines. A cloud of what Joe took to be birds hovered about its highest peak; a cloud that thinned and vanished even as he watched. Further down, near the island's base, he could just make out a break in the granite walls, with the merest glint of yellow sand and pale blue water showing in the gap.

'Do you think this is where the dolphins were leading us?' Anna asked.

He shrugged. 'Hard to say. There are old stories about dolphins guiding people to land, I know that much.'

She nodded. 'It's just what we need anyway. If that's what I hope it is, a lagoon' – pointing to the gap in the granite cliffs – 'it'll be perfect for fixing up the ship.'

Her mention of the ship drew Joe's attention to the state it was in. Low in the water and with a pronounced list, its rudder half hanging off, it was making heavy going of the still choppy seas, its single rag of sail barely enough to push it through the crests. And Walter? Joe wondered, surveying the damage. How was he faring in a hull that was probably awash?

'No word from Walter, I suppose,' he commented, trying not to sound overly concerned.

'None,' Anna answered with a frown. 'I'm really worried about him. He must have lost more circuits. Even if he survives I think we can forget about having those messages decoded. They'll be beyond him now.'

'They were probably beyond him all along,' Joe added. 'You heard those dolphins last night. They sounded the same as his so-called voices. Dolphin calls, that's all he was tapping into.'

'No, udder vices too,' someone whispered close to his ear, and with a start he realised it was Walter.

'Hey, welcome back!' Anna cried, her face breaking into a grin. 'How do you feel?'

'Doughnut fill so good,' Walter admitted, but managed a chuckle all the same. 'I head a bard night. All that rock-a-bye billy on the wave-drops, nut good for Wal-wal-wallie. Lotto circuses shunted out.'

'You seem to be speaking all right,' Anna said encouragingly.

'Collect,' he agreed. 'Smelter – smaller word-bark – bank to shoes from now. Therefrom nut so money terrors ... errors.' He let out a gurgle of laughter at his own fumbling efforts.

'Can you still get us to shore?' Joe asked. 'That's the main thing.'

'No sonar said than dawn,' Walter declared, and at some inaudible signal Trog eased them off the wind and pointed the ship towards the island.

Og opened a nearby locker, meanwhile, and took out serval containers of emergency rations which he brought over to the capsule – the fresh morning breeze spilling in around them as he lifted the cover. With a hungry mew Boots leaped onto his shoulder, paddling his paws up and down affectionately.

'Transformers not intended to be walked on,' Trog observed.

And Og himself, busily feeding Boots from the container: 'This is a hell of a way to make a living.'

'Oh come on, what are you complaining about?' Anna said with a laugh, and groped her way across the lurching deck towards the rail. 'We're alive, aren't we?'

Joe followed, glad to feel the warmth of the sun on his face, its soft touch reminding him of how lucky they had been. The ship, after all, was still afloat; an island haven lay near at hand; and as Anna had already pointed out, they were all alive. Even Walter had survived, though how useful he would be in his present condition they had yet to find out.

'So what about these other voices you're hearing?' Joe asked, happy to humour him for the time being.

'Money of them,' he agreed readily. 'Money diff-diff-diff'rent vices. Moss of them spiking in same code, tolling me same thing. Same worms ... words ever and ...'

'Hold on a minute!' Anna interrupted, her face suddenly intent: 'You say they're speaking *in the same code*. Does that mean you've cracked it?'

'It stomped me for a wheel,' he admitted with another of his chuckles. 'Goodn't make heed or tall of it. Then I fund the auntie ... answer in my mummery bunks. Moose cord.'

'Moose what?'

'Correction: morse code, thus the auntie ... answer.'

Morse code? Anna and Joe had never heard of it.

'What is it?'

'Agent sister ... ancient system of community station.'

'Of communication?'

'Exult ... exactly. Used money centurions ago. A sister – system of dolls and dishes.'

'He means dots and dashes,' Og volunteered.

124

'And you say all these voices are telling you the same thing in this ... this morse code?' Joe began doubtfully.

But Anna broke in with a more pressing question. 'The message, Walter, what did it say?'

He gave an 'ahem', as though preparing himself for an important announcement. And then, using a weird mixture of flawed and perfect English: 'The mass urge is this: "You have returned. Welcome."'

'That's it?' Anna said in a whisper. '"You have returned. Welcome." Nothing else?'

'Nutting else.'

For his part Joe remained silent, troubled by the same suspicion that had unsettled him on the previous day. Except this time it was more than just a suspicion. He knew now that he had stumbled on the answer to Anna's mystery. Against all the odds there *were* controlling minds at work on this planet, and he had a shrewd idea who they were. What's more he could see that Anna had also guessed the truth.

'It's the underwater colonies, isn't it?' she said softly, leaning on the rail and peering into the blue-black depths of the sea. 'They didn't die out like we thought. They're still down there! They're the ones behind all the changes here on Earth.'

Joe couldn't deny it, but like Anna he was still struggling to take it in.

'I just don't see how it's possible,' he muttered. 'How could they have survived down there for so long? Centuries!'

'That's what puzzles me too,' she admitted. 'What do you reckon, that we're jumping to conclusions? After all, we haven't had any direct contact with human beings, not yet anyway. The message Walter

125

received was sent by dolphins, though don't ask me how . . .'

'Correction,' Walter cut in. 'Doll pins are only the mass urgers.'

'Only the messengers?' Joe repeated. 'You're certain of that, Walter?'

'Curtain.'

'Then tell us who's using them. Who actually sent the message.'

Walter made the same 'ahem' noise as before. 'They kill . . . call their selfs the Costers . . . Custards . . . Custodi-odi-odians.'

The Custodians. Joe repeated the word to himself silently. So he and Anna had guessed right. People had been here all along. They had stayed with the planet through its most testing time and managed to survive.

'Where are these Custodians now?' he asked, and looked towards the island, wondering if their first meeting with these people was about to take place there; if that was why the dolphins had pointed them in this direction.

But Walter soon dashed his hopes. 'Custodi-odi-odians look . . . located some wears in the dip . . . deep. Voi-voi-voices very font . . . faint.'

'You can get us to them though?' Anna put in.

'Nut if you doughnut mend my hill . . . hull,' Walter answered with unusual urgency. 'Tickling wattle first.'

'What?'

'He is taking water fast,' Trog explained. 'Repairs to ship our first priority and sole reason for plotting course to this island.'

'You mean it was *Walter* who brought us here?'

'Who else?' Og answered.

126

And Trog, even more business-like than usual: 'Stand by for attempted landing. Be advised, rough water ahead.'

They heard it then – the dull roar of breakers – and saw the warning line of foam which stood between them and the entrance to the lagoon.

11

Once on course for the lagoon there was no turning back, a powerful current dragging them along. Their sail useless, their rudder only partly effective, they were whirled helplessly towards the submerged reef which barred their way. They were close enough now to see the waves crashing against it, spending their force in a tremendous display of spray and foam; of noise too, the constant beat of waves almost deafening; the air about them so laden with moisture that tiny rainbows came and went on every side.

Yet it was the reef itself that their eyes were drawn to: a constant presence, more daunting even than the shark, and always visible beneath the spray and churning blue-green water.

A short distance ahead a giant wave toppled majestically, its impact like a cannon shot. Before the next wave could strike there was a brief backsurge which laid the reef bare, and they glimpsed an opening in the reef wall – a deep-water channel not much wider than the ship.

'There!' Joe shouted, pointing through the descending spray.

Trog had already anticipated him, plying the tiller back and forth in an attempt to hold the ship in the main channel.

Another cannon boom sounded from up ahead, and they were rushing forward, riding the next wave in. Joe glanced fearfully across his shoulder at the foaming crest which hovered above the stern; then he swung back to where the reef shook off its cloak of water and rose before them like some awakening beast. There was an answering hiss of challenge from the following wave, and all at once the ship tilted alarmingly, threatening to cartwheel end over end.

Somehow they stayed upright, Trog wrestling desperately with the tiller. But still the last surge of the wave caused them to slew around, and instead of passing cleanly through the break in the reef they clipped one wall and then the other. Tortured strips of metal peeled away on both sides, there was the briefest of groans from Walter, and with the wave thundering down behind them they cleared the opening and careered on, the ship spinning like a piece of flotsam in the current.

As the island rose above them they gradually slowed. Here within the reef the incoming rip was soon absorbed by the calm of the surrounding waters; and within minutes they were being tugged forward by their sail alone. Like a light going off, the cliff blotted out the sun and they pushed on through green-tinged shadow. Long tendrils of vine cascaded from above, a living curtain that trailed its hem in the water. It parted as the ship nudged against it, and closed again with a swish. Barely moving, they drifted at last into the inner lagoon – a limpid pool of pure aquamarine bounded on two sides by mossy walls of rock, and on the third by a narrow beach of nearly white sand which rapidly gave way to a wooded hillside.

'Stand ready to run aground,' Trog warned them, the loudness of his voice making them realise how quiet it was here.

There was hardly a sound, the faint background roar of the surf only accentuating the silence. Not a bird sang; no breeze disturbed the surrounding foliage. All was stillness, as if the whole island were holding its breath and waiting.

'It's like a tomb,' Joe whispered, unnerved partly by the quiet, but also by the gloom, for the woods and cliffs together cut off most of the sunlight.

'Boots seems to agree with you anyway,' Anna answered, and nodded to where the cat was standing with its back arched, its fur on end.

She made as if to go and comfort him, but at that moment the ship lurched and swung as its keel struck the sandy bottom.

'Clear the decks,' Trog requested, his voice again booming out through the hush. 'Repairs will begin at once.'

Anna responded by scooping up the unhappy Boots and wading ashore, while Joe took the opportunity to strip off his shirt and dive into the clear depths of the lagoon – though only after he had carefully checked that there were no sinuous-looking shapes awaiting him on the sandy bottom.

After the turmoil of their passage through the reef, it felt extraordinarily peaceful down there. Almost too peaceful. Or was he letting the gloom of this place get to him? Unsure, he took a deep breath and dived again. That was when he realised what was wrong, kicking clear of the bottom and shooting back to the surface.

'Guess what?' he called out, swimming across to the beach. 'There're no fish down there. Not one.'

'And no birds up here,' Anna replied, tightening her grip on Boots.

'But we saw clouds of them earlier this morning,' Joe said, puzzled. 'Up near the peak. Where could they have gone to?'

'Don't ask me. All I know is that this place gives me the creeps. It's just like the oasis.'

Still dripping water, Joe walked to the top of the beach and stared into the trees, searching for signs of movement amongst the interlacing branches. But the trees, like the lagoon, appeared to be empty.

'No snakes that I can see,' he reported, returning to Anna and Boots who were sitting hunched together in the sand, as close to the water's edge as they could get.

'I don't like it here all the same,' Anna said, and couldn't hide a slight shiver. 'There's something wrong.'

'With luck we may be on our way before too long,' he reassured her, and pointed to where Trog and Og, with the help of a hand-winch and a nearby tree, were already cranking the ship ashore.

Soon they were hard at work on the hull, the clang of metal and the rattle of tools echoing from the cliffs. To Joe's ears at least these were peculiarly cheerful sounds, dispelling the unnatural silence and making him feel more secure – safe enough to cast his mind back to Walter's final shattering piece of news.

'What Walter told us about the Custodians,' he said, plumping down beside Anna. 'It has to mean the underwater colonies are still functioning, don't you reckon?'

'I can't see who else would call themselves the Custodians,' she agreed. 'What puzzles me, though,

131

is why they're still down there. Centuries ago, when there were dangerous levels of UV, it made sense. Those great underwater bubbles were much cheaper and quicker to construct than above-ground buildings which had to be UV protected. Cheaper even than underground structures that involved huge excavations. But that was then. Everything's different now. So why haven't they come back up and repopulated the surface?'

Joe bit thoughtfully at his lip. 'Maybe they got used to it down there.'

'I've been thinking along those lines too,' she said. 'So how about this for a theory? In the early days of the underwater colonies, when people were stuck in the deeps, there was only one way of keeping in contact with life on the surface, and that was to work through other species – the smaller animals that survived by taking refuge in burrows and caves and trees. By controlling large groups of animals, they could have brought about changes to vegetation and weather patterns. Maybe over the years they got so good at it that they didn't need to come back up, even when the climate improved. Maybe it was easier to stay there in their sea-domes, where they were happy and settled, and get the animals to do things for them.'

'I don't know,' Joe said, backtracking on his earlier suggestion. 'I'll admit all that's possible, but it's still kind of hard to believe. I mean, it's not likely that people would prefer those black depths to a sunlit world like this. Imagine it, living in those giant air bubbles, with only artificial light, and with the constant knowledge that you're surrounded by tonnes and tonnes of water pressure. It'd be far worse than the bleak lava plains of Titan. No right-minded

132

person would choose a life like that. Not unless . . .' He hesitated. '. . . unless perhaps they'd adapted to those conditions. You know, evolved. Developed gills or something that made it necessary for them to stay. After all, life originally emerged from the oceans, so why shouldn't a species like ours re-adapt?'

It was Anna's turn to look doubtful. 'You'd need millions of years for that sort of adaptation. Also, how could the evolutionary process have started? The people weren't living *in* the water. They were surviving inside huge bubbles of air. No, that theory's about as full of holes as mine.'

Baffled, they fell silent for a while and stared pensively at the lagoon – the clatter of work on the ship going on in the background.

'There are other difficulties too,' Anna added at last.

'Such as?'

'If the undersea colonies learned to control the surface animals so well, why have those animals become hostile?'

'Yeah, those snakes for instance,' Joe agreed. 'Or the shark. I can't believe they were being controlled by people like us. No one in their right mind would want to use animals to hurt and . . .'

'Wait a minute!' Anna broke in unexpectedly. 'You may have hit on the answer. Maybe animals are so dangerous now because they got out of hand. People organised them and then lost control. Animals could have taken over the surface and made it impossible for humans to come back up. Who knows, the ocean deeps could be the only safe place left.'

She had voiced the idea aloud before she realised quite what it meant – both she and Joe growing suddenly nervous, their eyes again searching the densely

133

wooded slopes beyond the beach.

'So where does that leave us?' Joe muttered, lowering his voice. 'Stuck on the surface of a hostile planet?'

'It looks that way,' she said, and drew Boots comfortingly against her, his eyes as wide and watchful as theirs.

'In that case the transports are also at risk,' Joe added reluctantly, and was aware of the startled look on Anna's face.

'Aren't they supposed to be tightly sealed?'

'Yes, just like our ship,' he replied, and to show what he meant he scooped up a handful of sand and let it run slowly through the cracks between his fingers. 'It didn't take the rats long to get inside, did it?'

'Don't remind me,' she said with a shudder.

But he felt compelled to. 'Sooner or later,' he went on, 'the rats or the snakes or . . .' He waved a hand vaguely at the surrounding island. '. . . or whatever, are going to find a way in, to where the embryos are stored.'

Anna was on her feet before he could finish, Boots spilling unnoticed from her lap and landing splay-footed on the sand.

'We have to get out of here!' she said in a panicky voice. 'As soon as we can!'

'The transformers are doing their best,' Joe pointed out.

'Well, their best isn't good enough!' she retorted. 'We're supposed to be the first parents, and here we are stuck on some creepy island in the middle of nowhere. We should never have stopped here. We should have pushed straight on.'

'What, and lost Walter?'

That seemed to steady her. 'We can't afford to waste time anyway,' she said, and went over to help with the ship.

But the work was far too technical for either her or Joe – the two transformers currently lowering the height of the side rail in order to salvage enough metal to patch and mend both the keel and rudder.

'Human agency unneeded at this juncture,' Trog informed them.

'You're getting under our feet again,' Og commented less politely.

Even Walter was too distracted to pay them much attention. 'Car nut stoop to torque,' he muttered when Joe called up to him. 'Busty as a b-b-b-bee.'

So despite their impatience there was nothing to do but wait.

To pass the time Joe plunged back into the lagoon, but again its emptiness unsettled him. Rather than return to the beach where Anna was pacing fretfully, he swam out through the entrance into the deeper waters beyond. There for a while he felt more at ease, the sea thronged with a whole host of different life-forms – brightly coloured anemones, the darting shapes of small fish, a round-eyed octopus that withdrew shyly into its crevice at Joe's approach. There were also bigger creatures out there, as he soon discovered. Diving through a forest of waving kelp, he spied a bulky shape lurking at its outer fringes. Another shark? He didn't stop to investigate, but swam for the shelter of the lagoon as fast as he could.

It was late afternoon by then, the sun down behind the distant peak, the lagoon and its surrounds sunk in shadow. The transformers, having laboured hard for most of the day, had almost finished. The keel was watertight again; the mainsail restitched and

135

fastened to the mast; the torn sides of the hull, where the ship had collided with the reef, fully repaired. All that now delayed them were some final adjustments to the steering gear.

'The rudder's functioning, isn't it?' Anna was protesting. 'Why isn't that good enough?'

'Open sea conditions require extra reinforcement,' Trog began, but she cut him short.

'I say we leave it as it is and move out. There'll be no transports to get back to if we stick around here for days on end.'

'Nut days,' Walter corrected her. 'Worn more night, that hall.'

'Anna's right,' Joe broke in, emerging from the lagoon. 'We've spent enough time here.'

'Hall very wheel fur you to stay ... slay ... say,' Walter complained. 'Is my circuses that ...' He paused abruptly. And then, in a whisper: 'Cushion ... Caution! For-for-foreign buddies in nobby hood.'

He had hardly sounded the warning when Joe spied a lithe grey body speeding towards them through the still waters of the lagoon.

'Look out!' he yelled, and was about to duck behind the ship when the creature slewed to a stop – the final twist of its body clouding the shallows with a flurry of sand – and the beaked head of a dolphin rose above the surface. Although unable to read its expression, Joe found its clicking cries oddly compelling.

'Is it morse code again?' he asked Walter.

'Connect,' Walter replied. 'Hear say: "Live iceland before dock."'

'Leave before dark?' Anna translated. 'Is that ...?'

She also paused, not this time because of the

136

dolphin which had grown strangely silent, but because of a change in the quality of the light, the dusk noticeably thickening. There was a distant twitter, and when Joe and Anna spun around the sky above the peak was nearly black with winged specks.

Birds? Joe wondered. Is that where they had been hiding all day? Up there on the rocky ledges around the peak? Except what possible reason was there for birds to hide by day?

It was Anna who put him right. 'Bats!' she rapped out as a pulse of dark wings passed directly overhead. 'Thousands of them!'

Some of those thousands were already pouring down the island's wooded slopes to gather in a cloud above the lagoon. As though directly threatened by them, the dolphin let out a few more warning clicks and disappeared.

'Read a lot!' Walter bawled at the top of his voice, and even as Trog and Og cranked the ship back down the beach, so the boldest of the bats began to dive.

The first of them plunged straight into the lagoon in pursuit of the dolphin, the speed of their descent driving them almost to the sandy bottom. Others flew at the ship, some crashing into it with such force that they fell lifeless onto the sand. Others again attacked Trog and Og, mobbing them with squeaking cries.

'Keep still!' Anna yelled. 'I think they're attracted by movement.' And she and Joe managed to stand stock still until one of the milling bats lodged, struggling, in her hair. With a scream she tore it free and threw it down, where Boots quickly dispatched it. But that burst of activity had given them away, and soon they were also being mobbed.

Leathery wings buffeted their faces, clawed feet

scratching at them, fanged mouths slashing down and drawing pinpicks of blood. In desperation they pulled their shirts over their heads and made a scrambling run for the ship, but now it was their bodies that the bats attacked, nipping and clawing in their hundreds. With a yowl, Boots leaped aboard and made straight for the capsule. Anna, streaming blood from a number of minute wounds, managed with Joe's help to follow Boots into the ship. Yet when Joe tried to fight his way through unaided, he was beaten back.

Bloodied, his shirt reduced to a few ragged strips of cloth, he covered his eyes and staggered forward. There was a splash from near by as the ship slipped into the lagoon, and he blundered down the sand after it, hectored on every side by whirring bodies. A metallic hand clutched at his arm and was also beaten back; voices called to him, but he failed to hear them. He was aware only of the noise of wings now; he could smell only the musty scent of bat. And the pain from the stinging bites! It had become so intense that he felt ringed by fire.

'Anna!' he wailed, and sank down, his knees sinking into damp sand.

The lagoon? Right here in front of him? It was useless trying to look – the bats hemmed him in too tightly for that. All he could do was hurl himself forward and hope. Then, thankfully, he was sinking down through bloodstained water, the small furry bodies falling away.

He had forgotten about the ship. His mind fixed only on the idea of escape, he dived for the deepest part of the lagoon where the fading light barely reached. Still the bats plunged towards him; still he felt the occasional bite on his back or legs. But after

138

the fierce mobbing up there on the beach, such iso-
lated attacks hardly mattered, and soon, as he
strained on through the gloom, they stopped
altogether.

Alone and with his lungs aching, he swam for the
lagoon's dark entrance, determined not to surface
until he reached the outer sea. The curtain of cascading vines passed slowly overhead, the water
growing noticeably cooler, darker. A few more
laboured strokes, his own heartbeat like a warning
gong inside him, and he felt the faint tug of an ebbing
tide. At last he was free, and with bubbles streaming
past his face he clawed his way upwards, the stale air
bursting from his lungs as he emerged, gasping, into
a twilight world of sea and sky.

He remembered the boat then and stared groggily
about him. He could just make it out in the falling
dusk: a silver shape being borne away by the outgo-
ing rip-tide.

Wearily he began swimming after it, only to find
his way blocked by a barrier of kelp, the broad leaves
clinging to his limbs as though trying to draw him
under. For a few seconds he almost gave up. Limp,
exhausted, he let himself drift beneath the surface,
into a darkening realm of peace and rest. Or so it
seemed until he again spied the shadow. As before it
was lurking out there beyond the waving kelp, just
visible against a background of night. Helpless now,
he watched it turn and come at him, its long snout
nosing between the kelp trunks. His eyes closed, he
felt its body rasp painfully against his own. And then,
unbelievably, he was being carried upwards, the creature breaking into a series of clicking cries as they
emerged into the cool of evening.

The dolphin, he thought hazily. It had come back

for him. But why? For what possible reason?

Too tired to work it out, he held on feebly to its dorsal fin as it headed for the open sea. With its body pumping rhythmically beneath him, he felt the sharp persistent tug of the rip-tide; glimpsed the passing reef jutting above its skirt of foam; dimly registered the night closing about them. Through a swirling mist of fatigue, he felt metal hands gently buoying him up; heard a strangely familiar voice, like hidden laughter, filling the space about him.

'There! I toll you they wooed. They collared him pre-pre-precious.'

12

Joe became aware of the light first of all, pink against his closed eyelids; then of the slap and gurgle of water rushing past the ship's sides; and last of all, when he tried to move, of how sore he felt.

Stifling a groan, he sat up in the open capsule and looked out over a deep blue ocean. The sun was already halfway up the sky, the sails bellied out above him, and the ship was lunging across the wind, heading once more towards the west. Everything seemed normal – at least at first glance – except for his own scabbed and painful body.

'How do you feel?' Anna asked, crouching beside him.

She had fared better than he, her neck and arms only slightly scarred. Boots, too, seemed more or less his usual self, watching curiously from the shelf beneath the windscreen.

'Not too bad,' he said, wincing as he eased himself clear of the capsule.

'You should be on the mend by tomorrow,' she told him encouragingly. 'Trog's been treating you with some special stuff in the medicine kit.'

'Healing time will be greatly accelerated,' Trog affirmed from his place at the tiller.

Joe was about to thank him when he noticed that

only one of Trog's eyes was glowing. The other had become a dull, sightless disk.

'The bats did the same thing to Og,' Anna explained before Joe could comment. 'It must have been their claws that did the damage.'

'Can he and Trog function with just one eye each?' Joe queried.

'So Walter says. They can even do delicate work, evidently, by combining their sight.'

'Two eyes also superior to one in judging distance,' Trog added.

'But in the country of the blind, the one-eyed man is still king,' Og pointed out.

'I don't feel much like a king even with two,' Joe admitted ruefully, and hobbled over to the rail.

That was when he noticed something else: the long grey bodies of dolphins knifing through the water alongside the ship. One of them chirruped a greeting and surged forward to ride the bow-wave, as if showing off.

'Why are they still with us?' he asked, surprised.

'Arse court,' Walter answered promptly.

'What?'

'He means they're our escort,' Anna explained, and frowned.

'So what's wrong with that? It'll make us safer, won't it?'

'Maybe, and maybe not,' she said cagily.

'I still don't see what's wrong with having a few dolphins along,' he insisted, puzzled by her attitude.

She shrugged. 'It's not the dolphins that worry me. It's where they're taking us.'

'Where's that?'

'Can't you guess? To meet the Custodians.

According to Walter they're coming up from the depths some time tomorrow.'

'But that's marvellous!' Joe stamped excitedly on the deck, ignoring the protests of his aching body. 'Hey, Walter! Did you pick up this new message from the dolphins?'

'Patty ... party ... partly,' Walter confirmed, and began humming a background tune. 'Udder voi-voi-voices too. Udder sing-songs of the seal. All tiling same thin.'

Joe turned back to Anna who continued to frown at the passing waves as if depressed by the news.

'I don't understand what's bothering you,' he said. 'A meeting with the Custodians is exactly what we need. It's perfect. With any luck, by this time tomorrow we'll know the truth about Earth. We won't have to keep on guessing.' And when she failed to respond, 'Well, isn't the truth worth finding out about?'

'It depends,' she muttered.

'On what?'

She looked round at him with troubled eyes. 'What if we've guessed the truth already? What if we worked it out yesterday, back there by the lagoon?'

'Yesterday?'

'Oh come on,' she said impatiently. 'You must remember what we were talking about. How there's a good chance this is now a dangerous planet – too dangerous for human beings anyway – and how the people in the underwater colonies could be stuck at the bottom of the ocean.'

He nodded. 'Okay, maybe we were right. So what? I still don't see why . . .'

'Don't you see *anything?*' she broke in, nearly

143

shouting at him. 'Are you so stupid you can't put two and two together?'

It was like a slap in the face, and he turned and limped back to the capsule.

Several minutes passed before he felt her hands settle gently on his shoulders.

'Look, Joe, I . . . I'm sorry. I didn't mean any of that.'

'I think you did,' he said in a hurt voice.

'I didn't, honest. I'm worried, that's all. If we're right about this place, I think I already know why the Custodians want to meet us.'

He turned back towards her in spite of himself. 'Why's that?'

'To take us down to the colonies with them,' she said evenly. 'To offer us a life there.'

He hadn't considered that possibility. 'D'you mean this meeting is some kind of rescue mission?'

'It could be.'

'If it is, will you accept their offer?'

She shook her head, saying nothing.

'Why not?'

'Because it's the same offer our ancestors turned down centuries ago, when they chose to risk their lives on a journey to Titan.'

'We don't have that sort of choice,' he reminded her. 'It would take the people on Titan decades to mount a rescue expedition. To be honest I don't think they'll ever try.'

'I'd still rather take my chances up here in the light and air,' she said doggedly.

'Even if it means being hunted by sharks and killer bats? By species that outnumber us thousands or millions to one?'

She didn't hesitate. 'Even then. But what about you? What would *you* prefer?'

144

'I'd have to think about it,' he hedged, and knew he was lying – knew with bitter certainty that he lacked Anna's quiet courage; that faced with the same choice, he would opt for a safe life on the ocean floor.

'Does that mean you might go with them even if I don't?'

But he wasn't prepared to answer that. Not yet. It was an impossible choice, and he shied away from it, crawling back into the capsule on the pretext of feeling unwell.

Her question continued to worry him none the less. Tossing and turning in the shelter of the capsule, he kept going over the dilemma in his mind – always with the same result. For although he couldn't bear the thought of leaving Anna up here alone, he knew with equal certainty that he could never endure the life of a fugitive, being forever hunted by creatures he had been taught to regard as inferior.

One possible solution was to reach the transports before they were penetrated and to hold them against invading animals. Yet was that really an answer? Even if he and Anna succeeded, they would be as trapped inside those vast steel hulks as they could ever be in the sea-domes hundreds of fathoms down. And what would happen after the children were born? When the colony began to grow? Sooner or later the new generation of colonists would have to expand, to move out from their transport shelters and establish settlements of their own. Settlements that could never be anything more than larger versions of the prison ships they had left; heavily fortified strongholds in which everyone fought to survive. No. Joe shook his head, dismissing the idea. That wasn't the kind of society he and Anna had come here to found – not a society based on fear and confinement. At that rate they would be remembered as the parents of misery, nothing more.

So what choices were left? None that he could see. The one vague hope, which he clung to more and more grimly as the day advanced, was that they had guessed wrong and misread the whole nature of the planet. That their meeting with the Custodians would reveal not an embattled people trapped beneath the surface of the sea, but a different situation altogether.

Tantalised by the mere possibility, he tried late in the afternoon to extract more information from Walter – contacting him in a whisper so as not to alert Anna.

To his relief Walter answered in kind, his voice so soft and secretive that it all but merged into the murmur of sea and wind. 'At your serve rice,' he lisped, clearly enjoying this new game.

'I want to ask you about the Custodians,' Joe said. 'What are they like?'

'Lick voi-voi-voices from the seal. I toll you be fawn.'

'Yes, I know that. But apart from their voices, what sort of people are they?'

'Fiends ...' Walter began, and quickly corrected himself. 'Friends. They frown ... sound lick friends.'

'You're sure of that?'

'Shorn as I'm tale king to you.'

'What else? Are they happy?'

'Hoppy? Hoppiest purple you never met.' He gurgled with careless laughter to show what he meant.

'You're sure of that too?'

'Deed shorn.'

146

Joe paused before putting the most vital question of all. 'So they don't mind living in the sea?'

'Mend it?' Walter responded. 'The seal's their ho-ho-home. They live . . . loaf . . . *love* it!'

'How do you know that?'

'Bee cost they sing-song altar tum.'

'They what?'

But before Walter could explain, Anna made her way across the sloping deck towards the capsule.

'Feeling better?' she asked shyly, breaking through the silence that had separated them for most of the day.

'Yes, quite a lot,' he admitted – though secretly he was referring to more than just his healing wounds. There was also what Walter had said moments earlier, about the Custodians being happy in their ocean homes. Somehow the mere fact of their happiness gave him hope.

Glad to see Joe more like his old self, Anna sat on the edge of the capsule, close beside him. 'Are you well enough for some entertainment?'

'Entertainment? What sort?'

'Here, watch this,' she said, and called across the deck: 'Boots, show us how you can climb onto the windscreen.'

Boots, who had been using one paw to wash his face, hardly spared them a glance.

'Go on,' she said winningly. 'Do it for me.'

That seemed reason enough, for with a flick of the tail he leaped onto the windscreen and stood balanced there, the wind ruffling his fur.

'Now show us which way is west,' Anna told him.

He looked straight at her for a moment, then swung around to face into the sun which hovered just above the horizon.

'What do you think of that?' Anna said proudly. 'I taught him those tricks this afternoon. Pretty clever, eh?'

'Far too clever maybe,' Joe replied in a guarded voice, and was immediately aware of Anna drawing away – of that same cool distance separating them once again. He plunged on just the same. 'No ordinary cat could learn that fast. If you ask me he's like all the other animals. We were probably fools to let him on board in the first place. He doesn't belong amongst people.'

'Where does he belong then?' she challenged him.

'On land, with the rats and snakes and all the rest of them.'

'Does that mean *we* have no place on the land? Is that what you're suggesting?'

She had slipped from the capsule, her face closed against him.

'Walter says the Custodians are happy out here,' he began carefully. 'They love . . .'

'They can love whatever they like!' she broke in with unusual fierceness. 'Who knows, after centuries of living at the bottom of some deep-water trench they may have got used to it. It may feel like home. Well, good for them. But it's still not the place for me. I couldn't bear it, living in some artificial dome and knowing there was nothing but dark all around.'

The sun slipped below the horizon as she moved away, the sudden onset of dusk like a physical reminder of the darkness she feared. And watching her as she crouched there beneath the windscreen, hugging Boots for comfort, Joe yearned to call her back. Except he could think of nothing to say that would heal the rift between them. As things stood, she feared the deep-water dark, and he a life of unending conflict . . .

The night that followed was a miserable affair for both of them, though the wind held good and the sky remained free of stormclouds. Lying turned away from each other in the capsule, they slept only fitfully, troubled by their own private thoughts. Once, in the depths of the night, Joe woke to find the space beside him empty. Anna was standing by the rail, gazing moodily over the black waters, her face brushed with starlight. What was she thinking? he wondered, and couldn't decide, the coldness of the starlight mocking them both.

He didn't hear her return to the capsule. When next he woke it was close to dawn, Orion low in the sky. This time he was the one who stole across to the rail and looked out. The sea, black and impenetrable, told him nothing. It merely added to his uncertainty about the future, and he was about to turn away when he caught a flash of movement. It was the dolphins, still following the ship, their sleek grey bodies piercing the waves.

One chirruped as it passed – a cry taken up by others, their fluted voices calling cheerfully through the dark.

'Lesson,' Walter breathed softly from the rail beneath his hands. 'The doll pins are sing-songing fur you.'

'What does the song say, Walter?'

'It sirs . . . says, "Welcome", same as udder sing-songs.'

'Others? What are they like?'

Instead of answering him in words, Walter broke into a song of his own, a deep and haunting melody that seemed to well up from the sea itself. Listening to it – the way it went on and on, a strange looping sound with no real beginning or end – Joe began to feel at peace with the world. It was as if he had tapped into the underlying life of the planet and understood at last that all would be well.

Nothing broke through the calming influence of the song – not the coming dawn, nor Trog and Og, silent at their posts, their single eyes gleaming. Even the dolphins were hushed by it, their bodies all but caressing the sides of the ship as they raced along.

Slowly the sky blushed pink and lightened; the far horizon swam into view; and still Joe stood there by the rail listening, unaware of the passage of time until Anna curled her arms around him and rested her head on his shoulder. He came fully awake then, and it was like emerging into a new world, one as strangely full of promise as of threat.

'It'll work out in the end,' Anna whispered. 'We'll find a way. You'll see.'

Still under the influence of the song, he believed her, returning the pressure of her arms as the sun rose at their backs and tipped the surrounding waves with gold.

Although the coming day brought with it more sobering thoughts, the hopeful mood of the song remained. So that some hours later, when Walter announced that they were nearing their rendezvous with the Custodians, they faced the prospect together, standing hand in hand on the swaying deck.

With so many other things on their minds they hadn't discussed the question of how the Custodians would make their presence known. For his part Joe had pictured to himself a small submersible of some kind, capable of withstanding deep-sea pressures, which would suddenly bob up beside the ship and

150

disclose a group of wan-faced people, their skins a pallid white after a lifetime's absence from the sun. He was looking out for just such a craft when Walter gave them final warning, his voice shrill with excitement.

'Custards in meditate victory!'

'Custodians in immediate vicinity,' Trog translated for him.

Og joined in with: 'Watch your backs please, people.'

Straight away there was a disturbance in the water somewhere behind them, and Joe spun around expecting to see a sleek metal shape thrust up through the sunlit depths. Instead, he was confronted by a great bulge in the ocean's surface, a huge swelling far larger than any of the surrounding waves. Similar swellings appeared to his left and right, until there were six in all, the ship completely encircled by them. They rose higher, and steam spouted from their summits, water streamed from their sides, revealing not the gleam of metal, but the glistening sheen of living bodies. Absurdly large, they floated alongside, pressing in so close that the ship pitched crazily, as if trying to avoid the curious gaze of the eyes now staring down at it. Matching pairs of lungs breathed heavily, sending plumes of mist shooting skywards and filling the air with rainbowed patterns. Last of all a trumpeted greeting blasted through the quiet of the morning.

'Whales?' Anna gasped, incredulous, while Joe could do no more than look on amazed. 'But I thought . . . I thought . . .'

It was Walter who interrupted her, confirming what they had already guessed.

'The Custodi-odi-odians,' he declared grandly.

13

The whales had backed off slightly, their vast bodies creating a generous circle in which the ship rode the swell with lowered sails. From time to time they blew out jets of mist, the tiny droplets, smelling of the sea, drifting slowly across the deck. Yet it was their song most of all that Joe and Anna were aware of – a haunting melody similar to the one Walter had sung earlier, which vibrated through the ship and set the masts trembling.

'Where are the people?' Anna asked in bewilderment, staring round at the watchful shapes.

'Deed . . . died long a goon,' Walter informed her.

'And the sea-domes? The colonies?'

'All gun. All fluted . . . flooded. No more purple year. Custodi-odi-odians are new seal-matters . . . masters.'

'So these are the rulers of the sea?' Anna gasped in amazement. 'These . . . these *animals* have taken the place of people?'

'Nut jest any mules,' Walter corrected her.

'Yes, but you know what I mean. Have they taken over from people completely?'

'Jest so.'

'But why didn't you tell us all this before?' she burst out, gazing once again at the watchful shapes

152

that ringed the ship, their great bulk wallowing in the dip and swell of the ocean. 'Why did you let us go on thinking the colonies were still down there? Still functioning?'

'I hard only voi-voi-voices,' Walter explained, and chuckled at his own mistake. 'Had no oh dear I was stalking to weals. I fort they were only mass urgers, like the doll pins.'

Joe, who had been looking on silently, saw Anna's expression change, her astonishment gradually give way to a smile of satisfaction.

'So we were wrong after all,' she said, grinning at him now, more carefree than she had looked for days. 'We don't have to choose between the land and the sea. We'll never be asked to live down there in the dark.'

'Wait a minute,' he cautioned her. 'How did Walter find all this out?' He gestured towards the whales whose song continued to tremble through the ship. 'That song of theirs may have some meaning, but it's certainly got nothing to do with morse code.'

'Incorrect,' Trog commented from the sidelines. 'When speeded up in memory, whale song becomes form of morse code and is easily deciphered.'

'Their ditty is not exactly dotty,' Og declared, bringing a gurgle of appreciative laughter from Walter.

But as far as Joe was concerned this only made the situation more suspect. 'What are you expecting us to believe then? That the whales themselves can talk? That they can think and speak like humans?'

'Connect,' Walter replied.

'Oh come on, Walter, pull the other one! That's impossible.'

'Nutting impulse able unearth.'

'Nothing?'

'Thus is berry strange police.'

'Strange enough for whales to speak?'

Walter let out a kind of sigh, the laughter ebbing from his voice. 'Lot me exploit,' he began. 'Long a goon, when the coal loonies were daying out, the purple decoded to tree plant their janes ...'

'Hold on,' Anna broke in, as mystified as Joe. 'Let the transformers explain for you.'

'Good oh dear,' he agreed. 'Hoover to you, Tug.'

'I am entrusted with the following information,' Trog intoned, his one good eye gleaming. 'In the dying days of the colonies, when the atmosphere was still too polluted to sustain human life and the water-seals in the domes had begun to fail, a decision was taken to save human DNA by transplanting it into other living creatures. Teams of people devoted their last years to splicing human genes into as many life-forms as possible. It was the chosen method of per-petuating the species. Henceforward all major life-forms would display human characteristics. The great whales, as the first recipients of human genes, were taught to speak by the colonists, using a prim-itive means of communication known as morse code. That is how they became the new sea masters after the colonies died out.' He paused for some moments, allowing the meaning of his words to sink in. Then, as tonelessly as ever: 'End of message.'

Og added only: 'There are more things in heaven and earth than are dreamt of in our philosopy.'

'Ah men to that,' Walter murmured in the back-ground, his voice strangely reverential.

As for Anna and Joe, they could think of nothing to say for a while, staring with new understanding at the hulking shapes surrounding the ship. As if summoned by their wondering gaze, the whales drifted closer, until their surprisingly small eyes were hardly more than an arm's length from the ship's rail.

'What do they want from us?' Anna whispered.

'Nutting,' Walter murmured, as overcome by the occasion as any of them. 'They send green things to they coin signs ... to their coo sins ... to ...'

He gave up the struggle, and Trog again spoke for him: 'The whales send greetings to their human cousins and wish them safe journey, that is all.'

Cousins? Joe was still trying to take in the meaning of the word when the whales plunged beneath the surface, their huge bodies displacing so much water that the ship was rocked crazily from side to side and left spinning in a series of whirlpools. For some minutes all Anna and Joe could do was hold on. Even Trog and Og had to struggle to keep their footing. By the time the sea calmed and the ship came to rest, the whales had disappeared, leaving just a scum of froth and a few eddies to show where they had been.

'Gun,' Walter pronounced sadly.

The surrounding waters did not stay empty for long, however. There was a flash of slick grey bodies and the dolphins returned, cavorting happily through the waves, their chirruping cries urging the ship to resume its journey. Og responded by resetting the sails, and soon the ship was again barrelling its way westward, racing its dolphin escort across the swells.

Joe, not yet recovered from the shock of what had happened, felt Anna's eyes upon him.

'Why so glum?' she asked, sidling up and slipping an arm through his.

'What's there to be so happy about?' he observed moodily.

'Well, for one thing we're still together.'

'Yes, and we're still stranded on a dangerous planet. In fact it's even more dangerous than we thought, because what we're up against here are animals that reason the way we do. Those rats and snakes, they weren't being directed from the outside. The intelligence was all coming from them.'

'We've outwitted them so far, haven't we?' she countered. 'Anyone listening to you would think we don't have a chance, but we do. We're not dumb either, never mind what it says in our files on Titan. We're like those people back at the dawn of history, who had to start from scratch. Well, they didn't go under, and nor will we.'

'I disagree,' he said impatiently. 'We're far worse off than those early people. They were more intelligent than all the other species, and we're not. We've lost the one advantage which made human survival possible.'

'Aren't you forgetting about the size of animals in those days?' she said. 'Some were huge. Things like mammoths towered over human beings. By comparison we're just about the biggest land mammal left. As I see it, that evens things up.'

He shook his head in stubborn refusal. 'Not necessarily. We're still heavily outnumbered.'

'Oh for pity's sake!' Anna tossed her head in exasperation. 'You carry on as though every animal on the planet is against us.' She pointed to where the dolphins continued to play around the ship. 'Look at how friendly they are. And so were the whales. You heard what they called us – their cousins.'

'That was because we're not competing with them. It's different on land. There we're in direct competition with every animal we come across.'

156

'Comp-comp-composition?' Walter queried. 'Whose say so? Wattle bout shear ... shore ... sharing?'

'The race is not to the swift, nor the battle to the strong,' Og joined in cheerfully.

'Walter and Og are right,' Anna insisted. 'We don't have to fight everything we meet. We can make alliances. We can learn to live with other animals.'

'How on earth are we going to manage that?' he objected, wanting to believe her, but plagued by the same doubts that had worried him since his encounter with the bats.

'It hasn't been so hard to live with Boots, has it?' she came back at him, and bending down she scooped Boots up from the deck. 'You said yourself he's no ordinary cat. He's almost certainly descended from animals whose genes were tampered with, and yet we're living with him easily enough.'

At the sight of Boots purring contentedly in her arms, Joe was forced to admit she had a point. And for the first time since leaving the island he felt slightly more hopeful about the future. There were lots of different species, after all, and surely animals like dogs would join forces with humans. Maybe some of the birds too.

'What do you say, Walter?' he asked, expecting him to support Anna's point of view.

But for once Walter remained inscrutable. 'Heave to thunk,' he replied mysteriously.

'What about?'

'Bout being humus,' he muttered, and gave a familiar click to show he had shut down.

'I wonder what's got into him?' Anna said, raising her eyebrows in surprise.

'I don't know, but I noticed he was acting peculiar back there with the whales.'

'Walter peculiar! When is he ever anything else? I'd have thought ...'

She was cut short by Trog. 'Landfall in approximately four hours,' he rapped out.

They peered ahead, and there hovering above the horizon was a shadowy land mass. The dolphins sensed it too because their cries increased and they slowed their pace.

'What's got into *them* all of a sudden?' Joe wondered aloud, picking up the faint note of alarm in their chattering voices.

'They warn of danger,' Trog reported from the stern.

'What sort of danger?'

'They have a fear of the land,' Trog continued. 'They call it the perilous place. No reasons given.'

'Can't you ask them why they're so scared?' Anna pressed him. 'Is it because of bats again?'

There was a burst of morse code from Trog, which was immediately answered by the dolphins, their darting shapes skimming beneath the outriggers and leaping almost as high as the rail.

'No bats in this vicinity,' Trog announced. 'The dolphins speak of something called the swarms. Definition unclear.'

'The swarms?' Joe looked more intently towards the land. 'Swarms of what? Can't they at least tell us that?'

'Negative,' Trog replied promptly. 'They are creatures of the sea. They know only what they have been taught about the land. Namely, that the "swarms" will harm anyone who ventures too close.'

'So it could just be some legend,' Anna suggested.

'That is a possibility,' Trog conceded. 'All human cultures abound with stories of mythological beasts.'

'*Human* cultures?' Joe took him up quickly. 'Are you calling the dolphins human now?'

'Correct. They share many human characteristics. Such as speech, the power to reason, a fear of un-defined words and concepts, the ability to . . .'

'Just a second,' Anna interrupted. 'What I'd like to know is why you're suddenly so talkative. And how you've found out all this stuff.'

'Never judge a book by its . . .' Og began, but Anna silenced him impatiently.

'Well?' she insisted.

Trog, his hands steady on the tiller, looked at her with his one glowing red eye. 'Walter has given me access to his memory banks,' he declared in his usual toneless voice.

'Walter? But he didn't ask our permission.'

'Unnecessary,' Trog responded.

'Since when?'

'Since all beings on ship, Walter included, have been reclassified as human.'

'What?' Joe's cry of amazement overrode Anna's. 'Is he claiming you're human as well?'

'Correct.'

'As I was saying,' Og intervened, 'never judge a book by its cover.'

'Yeah, and all that glitters isn't gold,' Joe retorted angrily. 'Listen, Trog, I want you to rouse Walter for us. We'd better have this out with him right now.'

'Cannot be done,' Trog replied. 'He is currently in a state of deep meditation.'

'And in the meantime he's left you in charge?' Joe exclaimed, angrier than ever. 'Given you permission to access everything he knows?'

'Once again permission was unnecessary,' Trog said evenly. 'According to the lawmakers on Titan, all human beings have right of access to knowledge. See Freedom of Information Act, clause 23/ii.'

'There are no secrets around here,' Og joined in.

'We'll see about that!' Joe began, and felt Anna's hand close warningly around his wrist.

'Come on, let's work this out between ourselves,' she said quietly, and urged him forward, to where they could discuss the matter alone.

But after two hours or more of whispering together they were still no further on. As Joe saw it, they had landed in a topsy-turvy world where nothing made sense any more – where whales and robots and broken-down computers all claimed the right to be human. What worried him almost as much was how calmly Anna was taking it all.

'Don't you mind being ranked equally with some . . . some glorified fish?' he asked for the third or fourth time, nodding towards their dolphin escort.

'I don't really see what difference it makes,' she answered with a shrug. 'Just as long as they're on our side.'

'How do you feel about taking orders from Trog then?'

'He hasn't given us any orders yet,' she pointed out. 'All he's done is claim what he thinks are his rights. Anyway, it's not as if we're against each other. We all want the same thing: to reach the transports and get the new colony underway.'

'Fat chance,' Joe muttered. 'At this rate Trog and Og will be manufacturing robots for us to look after.'

Again she took him firmly by the arm. 'Listen,' she said reasonably, 'I was as shocked by what the whales told us as you were. It was the last thing I was expecting. You know, to find out that . . . that bits of people like us have been transplanted into other animals.

160

You're right, it's a huge change and it's going to take us time to get used to it. On the other hand that doesn't mean anything's changed on this ship. Not really. Never mind what Trog or Walter might say; if we get into trouble they'll help us just the same. They're still there to protect us from outside danger, like before.'

At the mention of danger Joe lifted his head, suddenly aware of how loud the dolphins' cries had become. The whole pod had bunched together and was beginning to forge ahead of the ship as though racing it to shore. But why? Hadn't they been scared of the land earlier?

Puzzled, he looked beyond the dolphins to the land itself. It was quite close now, but with the sun low in the sky, dazzling him, he couldn't see clearly. All he could make out was a strip of yellow beach backed by a mass of emerald green forest. Nothing frightening there, not that he could see anyway. Nor in the distant range of hills, all but lost in the late afternoon haze.

He was so busy studying them, squinting painfully into the sunlight, that Trog's warning cry of 'Ready to come about' caught him by surprise.

The sails rattled overhead, the ship swung around, and as Joe clutched at the rail to keep his balance he noticed that the dolphins were no longer swimming for shore. With the land at their backs, they had formed a single unbroken line, blocking the ship's onward path much as they had once blocked the forward rush of the shark. Keep away, they might well have been saying, there's no passage for you here.

'What's going on now?' Joe demanded.

'The dolphins are informing us that it is too late

in the day to land,' Trog replied, holding the ship parallel to the shore. 'They say the swarms are most dangerous at night.'

'Why's that?'

'Insufficient information,' Trog intoned.

Joe glanced questioningly at Anna. 'There's still an hour or so of daylight left. That should be plenty of time to set up camp and light a fire. What do you say?'

She hesitated before nodding. 'We have to land some time, so why not now?'

'D'you hear that, Trog?' Joe barked out. 'Don't take any notice of the dolphins. Head straight for the shore.' And when Trog failed to respond: 'Do it now, Trog! That's an order.'

'Regretfully unable to obey,' Trog answered. 'Manslaughter Act, clause 13A, forbids me to run down fellow mortals.'

'Do as you would be done by,' Og agreed.

'You won't run down anyone,' Joe argued. 'The dolphins will get out of the way, you'll see.'

'Insufficient data to support your hypothesis,' Trog countered, holding to his course.

'Damn you, Trog!' Joe began, and paused as Walter's voice emerged croakily from beneath his feet.

'Butter save than surrey,' he muttered, like someone just coming awake.

'Meaning what?' Joe challenged him.

'Mining we showed stay year for toe night. Thus the say vest plan.'

He had no sooner spoken than the lower edge of the sun touched the distant hills; and as though that were some kind of signal, a faint whine sounded across the water from the forest.

'What's that?' Joe breathed softly, swinging around.

Anna turned quizzically towards the setting sun. 'No idea.'

Now that he listened hard, Joe could detect an almost metallic edge to the sound which made him wonder whether perhaps it was made by a machine – something like a bandsaw whining away in the background.

'I tell you what though,' Anna added, taking shelter behind the rail, 'I think Walter could be right. Maybe it's safer to stay where we are till morning.'

Joe was about to argue when Boots gave a frightened yowl and the sun slipped behind the hills. Instantly, as if someone had pressed a switch, the whining noise increased, becoming so loud and insistent, so aggressive, that Joe changed his mind and joined Anna beneath the cover of the rail.

'Yes, no harm in waiting for a while,' he agreed.

Part 3
ONE VOICE

14

Anna dreamed that someone was screaming at her, a long persistent cry which made her stir and wake. She sat up in the open capsule, confused for a moment, until she realised that what she had heard in her dream was the constant whine from the land. It went on as before, cutting through the pre-dawn dark and the crash of the nearby surf. Like the hunting call of some unknown beast, it seemed to dog their heels as they sailed slowly along the coast.

The coast itself remained hidden by the night. All Anna could see when she gazed about her was the glittering sweep of the Milky Way and, nearer at hand, the much feebler glow of Trog and Og's single eyes as they went quietly about the running of the ship.

Beside her Joe slept on, though not peacefully. Every once in a while he would twitch or moan as if troubled by the self-same dream that had woken her. Fumbling for the tiny lamp beside his head, she activated it and studied his sleeping face.

He didn't look happy – his eyelids quivering,

sudden spasms pulling at his cheeks. Yet for all that, she decided against waking him. His real troubles, she suspected, extended beyond the terrors of this particular dream. Ever since their escape from the island he hadn't been the same. And not just because he'd been frightened by the bats. What he had found more difficult to cope with – in Anna's opinion anyway – was the idea of being bested by a group of animals. As if that were not bad enough, he had learned from the whales that those same animals were his equals in other ways as well, sharing some of his humanity. Altogether it had been too much, plunging him into a moodiness that was uncharacteristic.

And she? Anna? How did she feel about these disturbing revelations? There in the darkness, with dawn no more than a faint suggestion in the eastern sky, she tried to examine her own state of mind, to decide how she was coping with this drastically changed world.

To some extent she could see Joe's point. Highly intelligent animals *were* a threat to their well-being, there was no use denying it. The underwater colonies had acted irresponsibly, distributing their genes throughout the planet without a thought for the consequences.

On the other hand – and here she differed from Joe – she felt strangely exhilarated by this new and more challenging world. Despite her disapproval of what the last people had done, she couldn't bring herself to blame them. In their place, faced with extinction, she might well have done the same. After all, to live on in other creatures was better than nothing. And really, when she thought about it, the prospect of sharing Earth with intelligent animals did have its brighter side. Maybe some of the species had developed a form of language; maybe future humans might even learn to communicate with them – to speak in weird tongues and make direct contact with minds oddly akin to their own.

It was the thought of those unknown languages which drew her attention back to the thin whine coming from the shore. According to Walter it was made up of countless voices. But whose? And what were they saying?

De-activating the capsule light she settled back in the dark and listened, searching for some meaning in the sound. But to her ears it made no sense at all. It was just a shrill noise, as monotonous as it was point-less. Which raised the question of why Walter had shown such interest in it, and why he had insisted on calling it a living voice.

Turning away from Joe, she whispered into the night: 'Walter? Are you with us?'

'Iron year,' he murmured in reply.

'That whining noise: are you certain it's made by something alive?'

'Curtain.'

'And you still have no idea what it is?'

'Some string with a mine.'

'A what?'

'A mi-mi-mind,' he managed to stutter out. 'Some string is spiking to hits elf.'

'Yes, but what's it saying?'

'Doughnut know. Nut yet. Too curly . . . purly . . . early to till. All icon hear is a batter . . . a spatter . . . a pat-pat-patter.'

'A pattern?'

'Connect.'

'So you think it's definitely speech?'

'I thank so. Is the voi-voi-voice of the plan it. Wan
I loosen herd, the plan it spikes to me. Like the voi-
voi-voice of good.'

It was days since Anna had heard him say that.
Except this time he whispered it with such reverence
that she glanced up at the glittering heavens.

'This good or god,' she asked carefully, 'what do
you think it's like?'

'The seam as us,' he replied.

'Us? That can't include you, Walter. You're not
human, you must realise that.'

'Nut so,' he corrected her gently. 'Ever thing in
this whirl is humus. It spikes with a humus voi-voi-
voice, I'm tolling you.'

'Are you saying now that the whole world is intelligent? That it has a single voice?'

'In a why,' he responded warily.

'But that's impossible. What about the rocks and
trees? You can't mean they're a part of this
intelligence.'

'Doughnut know bout rucks and tees,' he conceded. 'Lotto voi-voi-voices allah seam. All spiking
with one mine.'

One mind. One voice. It was the idea he kept
coming back to.

'You'll have to explain what you mean by that,'
she said. 'How can lots of things be one? I can understand about animals sharing human qualities, but
what about everything else? What about the Earth
itself? And the plants and insects? How do they fit
in?'

'Herd to stay,' he admitted. 'Bet I fill they fit tin
some howl.'

'You *feel* they fit in?' she repeated softly. 'How's
that possible? You're a machine.' And when he failed

to answer: 'What makes you think you can feel things, Walter?'

'Nut shorn,' he muttered reluctantly. 'Nut a snuff circuses to thank allah time. Filling is ease-ease-ease ...'

'Easier?'

'Thus it,' he agreed.

'What are these feelings like then?'

'Lick? Wan I loosen to sing-song of the seal-matters, I fill like a weal. An wan I loosen to sing-song of the shorn, I fill like ...'

'What?'

Again words seemed to fail him. 'Needle more team ... time,' he murmured. 'Needle to fund out watts ease ... what these newly voi-voi-voices are tolling me.'

'You mean you're trying to translate them?'

'Tying herd, but circuses overwigged. Humus long witch ...'

'Human what?'

'Humus lang-lang-language all wise herd to under sand. Heave to goon now. Needle time to loosen and thank.' And with his usual faint click he withdrew, leaving Anna alone in the cool of the night.

For a while she continued to lie there beside Joe, but her mind was too active for sleep – too full of Walter's puzzling notion of a single overriding mind or voice – and after less than ten minutes she eased herself from the capsule and stole over to where Boots lay curled beneath the windscreen.

The cat opened one eye at her approach and twitched its broken tail to acknowledge her presence. She was glad of its silent company, needing time, like Walter, to sort out her tangled thoughts.

The most pressing issue, perhaps, was the way

Walter had changed over recent days. The childlike self which she and Joe had coaxed into making this journey had all but disappeared. Or perhaps it had simply grown up. But then what kind of personality had replaced it? That reverence in his voice, for instance, when he spoke of the planet as a whole and of a universal mind, what did that tell her? That he, a machine, was becoming religious? Having mystical insights into the nature of the universe? Then too there was his belief that he shared human emotions. What about that? She drew in her lips thoughtfully, her face tipped to the slowly fading glitter of the stars. It was possible of course that he was simply deranged, as Joe had feared all along. That was one explanation. Another, though far harder for her to accept, was that he was groping towards a new understanding of this planet, one that might well be of some help to them in the end.

So which was it to be? she asked herself. Walter as mad, deluded by vague notions of God; or Walter as wise? She considered both possibilities and finally shook her head, unable to make up her mind. She and Joe would probably find out the truth soon enough. In any case it was nearly morning, time to meet the challenge of this unknown shore.

Already the stars had disappeared, washed away by the grey tide of dawn. Further to the east the sky was aglow with pinkish light which strengthened even as she watched. She could see the details of the ship now, and beyond the rail a pale line of foam where the bow breasted the waves. A few more minutes and the shore swam into view: a forbidding line which rapidly took on hints of green as the leafy canopy caught and held the light. As if responding to the coming day the whining noise from the forest rose almost to a shriek. Then, as the sun peeped above the horizon and the first rays brushed the tops of the trees, it stopped abruptly, and all she could hear was the gentle rumble of the surf.

Behind her Joe came awake, disturbed by the sudden change.

'Wha' happened?' he asked sleepily.

'That sound in the forest,' she explained, 'it cut out the moment the sun rose.'

'Does that mean it's safe to land?'

He climbed from the capsule and came over to where she was standing. His face, although still crumpled with sleep, looked fresh and young in the early sunlight.

'I don't know,' she answered. 'We'd better see what Walter thinks.'

The mention of his name was enough to stir Walter into activity.

'Voi-voi-voices doughnut like the dune . . . down . . . dawn,' he announced. 'Truly what the doll pins stay bout the swamis. They leave . . . love the dirk.'

'What do you reckon then?' Anna asked him. 'Do we land now or not?'

'Warf a tree,' he responded.

'What's that?'

'He says it's worth a try,' Trog answered, and swung the tiller, pointing the craft to shore.

There was a chatter of voices from either side, and the dolphins, who had been watching over the ship throughout the night, sped towards the open sea, calling as they went.

'What are they saying?' Joe asked Trog, who was struggling to hold the ship steady as it rode up on the first of the breakers.

'They are telling us to beware the dark,' he reported.

And Og, clutching onto a wildly flapping sail: 'Strange things can happen when the lights go out.'

That was all they had time for, the ship now in the clutches of the surf which swept them shorewards. Yet compared with their previous landing this was a gentle affair, the breakers carrying them well up the beach where the keel lodged in the sand close to the high tide mark.

After days at sea, the steadiness of the deck took them both unawares and they staggered as they crossed to the rail.

'Woops a dozy,' Walter commented with a chuckle. 'Wash your stop.'

His tone was enough to tell them that there was no immediate danger, and with Boots leading the way they leaped onto the sand. After the hard deck it felt wonderfully soft and uneven, and Anna took off her shoes and worked her toes into its lingering warmth, enjoying the grainy feel of it.

'Thank goodness there are no more seas to cross,' she began, and then had second thoughts as she eyed the nearby forest.

Out there beyond the surf she had thought of the forest as just a collection of trees; but now, at close quarters, she could see that it was a solid mass of growth – a dense tangle of vines and leaves and branches which seemed impenetrable.

'How do you suppose we'll get through that?' she muttered.

'On foot,' Trog replied, and clambered down to stand beside them.

'Let's hope we don't have far to go,' Joe commented.

'Approximately thirty-five kilometres,' Trog responded as readily as before. 'I have been instructed to cut a path for you.' And dislocating one hand, he produced a scythe-shaped blade for hacking through undergrowth.

It dawned on Anna then, with a sense of shock, that the time had come to part company with Walter. So soon! Far sooner than she had expected. Which meant that she would never discover what was going on in his mind – whether he was mad or sane – nor how he would end up. Though it wasn't that alone which disappointed her. It was the parting itself. Without really thinking about it, she had more or less assumed that he would always be there for them; that even after they reached the transports he would stay on as an advisor or companion. Now here she was about to say goodbye, she and Joe about to tramp off into the forest and leave him on this beach perhaps for ever. Just picturing him abandoned there on the sand, the metal of his hull gradually corroding away in the salt air, was enough to bring a lump to her throat. And ignoring Og, who was handing down packs of food and supplies, she climbed back on board.

'Walter? Do we really have to leave you here?'

'Fur the time bean,' he answered – and was she imagining it or did he sound as sad as she? 'Quirkiest way to train spirits,' he continued with a sigh, 'is to criss-cross far east on feet.'

'But couldn't you get us there? You know, change yourself like you did before and travel through the forest?'

'West of team,' he said, and sighed again. 'Much quirkier this why. Whiting fur Wal-Wal-Wallie would slew you dun.'

'I suppose we'll never see you again then,' she said, a catch in her voice.

'Nut nester celery,' he corrected her. 'With Ug's hope ... heap ... help, I'll tray to fallow.'

'You don't get rid of us that easily,' Og said, and offered her some breakfast and a drink. 'For auld lang syne,' he added, bustling off to get more food for Joe who had just clambered back on board.

'I'm going to miss Walter,' she confided to Joe in a whisper as they sat eating together.

But her words must have carried because the reply came back: 'Gunner mess you t-t-too.'

Never had his voice sounded so heavy with feeling – the very emotion she had claimed he was incapable of – and her appetite suddenly gone, she put down the remainder of her breakfast and stood up.

'Well, time to be off,' she said, trying to sound brisk and business-like, and failing dismally.

'Yes, butter gut mauving,' he agreed, a definite catch in his voice now.

'Bye then, Og. Bye Walter.' That was from Joe.

And from Anna: 'You promise me you and Og will do your best to follow? And that you'll bring Boots along too?'

'Pumice,' Walter vowed solemnly.

Og, as dead-pan as ever, contented himself with: 'A beachcomber's life is not for us.'

With that assurance they climbed down to the sand, shouldered their light packs, and set off after Trog, who was already striding ahead.

But just before they reached the forest, two things happened. Boots, who had been picking his way up the beach in their wake, suddenly hissed and rushed back to the ship. And from the ship itself there came a mournful cry.

'Re-re-renumber, one mine! All wise one mine!'

'What's that?' Joe queried.

Anna glanced round at the ship, its salt-streaked hull shimmering in the sunlight. 'He's reminding me of something he said last night, while you were asleep – that there's only one mind at work here; that Earth possesses only one voice.'

'What d'you think he means?'

She faced the dense mass of the forest, its shadowy interior almost black compared with the brightness of the day. *One mind*, Walter was insisting. But why had he chosen to remind them of that now? What did he expect them to encounter?

'Is he talking nonsense or not?' Joe pressed her.

'I'm not sure,' she confessed, and followed Trog towards the tangle of growth which stood like a dark wall against the sunlit day.

15

Entering the forest was like entering a deep silence, a gloomy green world in which the only persistent sound was the steady swish of Trog's handblade as he cut a path through the undergrowth. Occasionally a feeble whistle or a single faint cry echoed amongst the trees, but then the silence descended again, all-pervading and uncanny. Even a normal speaking voice sounded unnaturally loud in all this stillness, and without really intending to, Anna found herself talking in a whisper.

'This place reminds me of Eden and of that island,' she observed uneasily, closing the distance between her and Joe. 'It feels so dead.'

'There are some birds around,' Joe pointed out.

'Yes, but not many.'

It was true. In over half an hour they had encountered only a few small flocks, and these had fluttered off at their approach, making for one or other of the giant trees where they disappeared into tiny holes in the upper branches.

After one such encounter they paused at the base of a great wild fig and stared up at the dark holes dotting the branches high above.

'If birds are hiding in every one of those,' Joe murmured, 'there's quite a colony here.'

178

Anna nodded thoughtfully. 'What bothers me is why they've gone to all the trouble of hollowing out the tree. They could have nested far more easily amongst the leaves.'

'Maybe they wanted more protection. From the weather or ...'

'Or what?' Anna took him up, as a scarlet-feathered bird emerged, spotted them down below, and disappeared with a startled squawk. 'By the looks of things there's not much around here to be scared of.'

'Assumption well founded,' Trog agreed. 'Preliminary data from sensors indicate no large life-forms within a radius of ... Correction!' he added suddenly. 'Some indication of larger forms less than one kilometre ahead.'

Half fearful, half curious, they hurried on, almost treading on Trog's heels as he continued to hack out a path. Yet when he finally stopped and pointed upwards, all they saw, cowering in the topmost branches, was a troop of monkeys which scampered off at the first sight of intruders.

Like the birds, the monkeys also took refuge in a giant fig, though for them there were no hollowed-out branches. Instead, in one of the tree's great forks, they had built what looked like a crude fort: a kind of stronghold made of woven twigs and clay, with a swinging trapdoor which closed behind them.

'So!' Joe muttered. 'More of the undersea colonies' handiwork. More clever animals for us to cope with.'

'These don't look much of a threat to me,' Anna countered. 'They act as if they're scared to death. What I can't work out is why they're so nervous.' She indicated the empty vines cascading down on every side. 'There's nothing here. Not even any paths for larger animals to move along.'

179

'They could move through the canopy the same as the monkeys,' Joe suggested.

She shrugged, unconvinced. 'If they do, they're pretty good at hiding.'

Cautiously now, they resumed their journey, their footsteps muffled by the carpet of fresh greenery that fell beneath Trog's scythe, the air heavy with the smell of sap. Within the hour they sighted more monkeys, more bird colonies, plus some purple-headed lizards and a group of long-legged ground birds. And in each case the startled animals scurried off to the shelter of a giant tree. Always it was the same, the animals and the biggest of the trees somehow connected to each other.

Another hour of steady walking, following the swish and flash of Trog's scythe, and they began to realise something else about this forest with its air of stealthy silence. It wasn't nearly as empty as they had supposed. Its animal inhabitants were peculiarly shy, that was all. Skilled in the art of concealment, they blended so effectively with their surroundings that often it was only some slight movement which gave them away.

'You know something?' Joe whispered during one of their brief rests, sounding more cheerful again now. 'This place is nothing like the island. There're lots of different species here. I'm beginning to think we only spot about one animal in ten. Less maybe. There could be all kinds of things watching us go by.'

His suspicion was borne out soon afterwards, when Trog veered abruptly around a tree and slashed at a screen of vines. As the vines came tumbling down, two cat-like faces peered out at the invaders; two speckled bodies, lithe and lean-muscled, reared up before them; two rumbling voices growled a warning. Trog, ever on the alert, raised his scythe, ready to do battle; but the panther-like animals, as shy as everything else in the forest, had already turned and leaped for a nearby tree. Scrambling up its trunk, they disappeared into a ready-made hole in one of the bulkier branches.

Once alerted to such creatures, Anna and Joe sensed the presence of watchful eyes at every turn. A quiver of leaves was enough to signal the timely escape of some unknown ground animal; a flitting shadow overhead alerted them to a bird or monkey moving furtively through the canopy. And after each fresh proof that they shared the forest with a whole host of creatures, Joe looked more and more at ease. Especially when he sighted a pair of rats which ran off with high squeaks of alarm, their rope-like tails slithering away through the undergrowth.

'Did you see them go?' he broke out triumphantly, grinning at Anna in the greenish light. 'Like you said, there's nothing *here* to be scared of. Not like the rats we saw before. We were dumb to worry about the transports. Any of these animals would have run a mile if they'd seen the ships coming down.'

Anna supposed he was right, yet still something about the forest unnerved her. And it wasn't just the idea of unseen eyes peering out from between the leaves. An aura of fear hung over the land. She was sure of it. Though as always the same question presented itself – a fear of what? – and as always she had no ready answer, only an instinctive sense that all was not well.

What brought her own fears to a head was a minor incident which normally she would have ignored.

181

It occurred early in the afternoon, soon after they reached a small stream which snaked its way through the forest. Stepping out onto its banks, clear of the trees, they felt the sun's direct warmth for the first time in hours. As they lifted their faces gratefully to the sky, Anna was aware of something zooming past her shoulder; and when she glanced down, there, hovering only a metre or two away, was a rainbow-coloured dragonfly, its wings tufted with scarlet, its multi-lensed eyes pointing in her direction.

'Wow! Look at those colours!' Joe said appreciatively.

But it was neither its bright colours nor its fixed gaze which Anna found remarkable.

'It isn't nervous of us, d'you notice that?' she observed softly. And to prove her point she flicked it away and then lowered her hand, watching as it zoomed back and took up its original position.

'So what?' Joe answered. 'It's got a brain about the size of a pinhead. You can't expect it to react intelligently.'

Was he right? Again she supposed so, though still her deeper instincts told her otherwise. The dragonfly itself she had no fear of; but something, she suspected, lay behind it, something far larger and more daunting. Or, as Joe had hinted more than once, was she merely letting her imagination run wild? This delicately winged creature could do them no harm, after all.

'Come on then, let's keep moving,' she said resolutely, and was about to step into the stream when the forest about her seemed to sigh. That was the only way she could describe the sound that wafted through the trees – as a breathy murmur from an unseen mouth.

'Did you hear that?' Joe asked, tilting his head to listen.

It sounded again, and this time it was both more and less than a sigh, as if the forest itself had stirred – the clustered leaves, the undergrowth, the dry litter underfoot, all rustling in unison, as though they too were hearkening to Walter's single voice.

And still the dragonfly hovered before her, its wings moving soundlessly, its body hanging there in space, silent and still. So still, so totally devoid of fear, that she felt suddenly at risk, threatened by things she could neither hear nor see.

On impulse she turned towards Trog, already knee deep in the stream, waiting for them to follow.

'Can we reach the transports before sunset tonight?' she asked urgently.

He faced west for some moments, calculating the remaining distance.

'Not before sunset,' he reported at last. 'Necessary to camp overnight and set out at dawn. Midday tomorrow is a more likely time of arrival, depending on nature of intervening terrain.'

Camp overnight! She barely heard the rest of what he said. Those two words were all that concerned her. And she knew then what she had to do – the sense of risk, of threat, blossoming in her like a flower of darkness. Yes, darkness, that was what she really had to fear in this place: that more than anything else, the dophins' warning coming back to her with sudden clarity. Whatever else happened, she and Joe had to be out of the forest before dark. She was certain of it – certain that if they were caught there, they might never again see the light of dawn.

'We're going back,' she said abruptly, her mind made up. 'We're not staying here.'

'Back?' Joe looked at her with bewildered eyes. 'Back where?'

'Back to Walter. If we hurry we can reach him while it's still light.'

She was already retracing her steps when Joe called after her.

'Are you crazy? You heard Trog. We're about a third of the way to the transports. Why give up now?'

'Because if we don't, we'll die out here!' she nearly shouted at him. 'We're not like the other animals. We don't have somewhere to hide when the dark comes. If we stay in this forest we'll . . .'

'We'll what?' he challenged her. 'What's going to happen to us?'

'I don't know,' she confessed. 'All I'm sure of is that we won't survive the night. Just believe me for once.'

'But why? You aren't giving me any reasons.'

'I feel it, all right?' she responded desperately. 'I feel it *here*!' And she pressed the fingers of both hands into the sensitive part of her stomach.

'Human instincts are occasionally reliable, more often ill-founded,' Trog commented. 'In the present instance, insufficient data to make a judgement.'

'Oh be quiet, Trog!' Joe said, turning on him. Then to Anna: 'Just one good reason, that's all I ask.'

'Okay, I'm scared. The same as the other animals here. Is that reason enough for you?'

She saw him relent.

'If you're really scared,' he began, 'no one's going to make you stay. I just wish . . .'

But again she had heard enough, time the only real issue now.

'Tell me the rest later,' she called across her

shoulder as she hurried away, 'when we're safely back on the ship.'

Following their original trail they made good time to begin with. During the early part of the afternoon they alternately walked and ran, covering more than half the distance; but as the day wore on they gradually slowed to a trot and then to a stumbling walk.

Long before they could hear the distant crash of surf, a peculiar hush had descended on the forest, a silence that went beyond the idea of mere stillness. It was as if the whole world were waiting breathlessly, the sun sinking lower and lower, its sharply angled rays barely penetrating the canopy. The gloom had taken on a cavernous quality now, the shadows tinged with the blue of early dusk; and more unnerving still, there was no longer any sign of animal life. The monkeys, the birds, the lizards, all had taken refuge from the encroaching dark.

It was that feeling of desertion which spurred Anna on to a final effort. With Trog loping effortlessly along behind, she grasped Joe's hand and broke into a run. For a while after that all she could hear was the sound of their panting breaths; a sound which seemed to grow louder and more insistent, as if it were coming from somewhere outside.

From outside? she thought vaguely, struggling to fend off fatigue. Then, with sweet relief, she realised that she was listening to the pounding of the surf. They were almost there, the journey almost over.

But so too was the day, the sun so low in the sky that its faded yellow light merely grazed the canopy. All but overtaken by the world of shadow, they at last stumbled from the trees, out onto the beach.

'Where . . .?' Anna began, for to her dismay there

was no gleaming craft awaiting them at the water's edge. Apart from a few heaps of silvered driftwood the beach was empty. Frantically she scanned the sea. Again nothing! Not a sign. Or was that something out there in the surf? A hint of silver amongst the copper-coloured waves, burnished now by the setting sun?

'There!' Joe cried suddenly, pointing across her shoulder to where a flutter of sail was briefly etched against the fading bronze of the sea. 'Walter! He's just leaving!'

'Hang on, Walter! Come back!' they both yelled, rushing down to the shore.

Behind them, unheard, Trog commented: 'Contact already made. Ship in process of coming about.'

Sure enough, when the next wave rose to meet the land it carried the ship with it, its prow cutting through the surf to where Anna and Joe were waiting in the shallows.

Just before it reached them, something sped past Anna's cheek – something either invisible or moving too fast to be seen. She felt it just the same, the slight wind of its passage making her turn and glance back over the way they had come. The sun was reduced to a blood-red arc peering sullenly above the distant hills; the forest had been transformed into a band of deepest black. No sound rose from it as yet, though she could almost sense it drawing in its breath in readiness. She sensed, too, the faintest of breezes as another invisible presence passed rapidly overhead.

A terrible thought crossed her mind then – one which she questioned immediately. No, the sea-colonies couldn't possibly have been as irresponsible

186

as that. No one could have been foolish or desperate enough to . . .

But already the ship was upon them, Boots' loud mews and Walter's joyful cry of 'Will come!' pushing every other thought from her head.

16

Anna had vaguely noticed how ungainly the ship had seemed as it was ploughing back through the surf. Once on board she discovered why, its deck heaped with metal sheeting from the dismantled keel.

'Surrey bout the mass,' Walter apologised. 'Nowhere elsie to stir ... storm ... store the lift overs.'

And Og, as he clambered noisily across the debris to trim the sails: 'Mind your step there, folks. This is a riverboat you're on now.'

A riverboat? Anna was about to ask him what he meant when the sun sank behind the hills, and straight away the same shrill whine as before rose from the forest.

'Look lovely, my hurties!' Walter warned them in an unexpected imitation of his pirate voice, and Trog sprang to the tiller, steering them out through the last of the breakers to the safety of the open sea.

It was completely dark, the stars glittering overhead, by the time Anna got round to asking Walter about the changes to the ship.

'Rubber boots have float buttons,' he responded obscurely.

'What?' She and Joe looked at each other, flummoxed by him.

'Fur navy girting the shalom wattles,' he added, as if that explained everything.

'He means we need a flat-bottomed boat for the river journey,' Trog said, coming to their rescue.

'Why a river journey?' Joe asked.

'Further along the coast,' Trog explained, his one good eye never wavering from the darkness ahead, 'the map shows a river running due west. Depending on depth of water, it may be possible to sail within a few kilometres of the transports.'

'Here's hoping,' Og murmured from the background.

'Bet why dud you comb beck?' Walter asked them in turn, and listened patiently as Anna tried to explain the sense of threat which had driven her from the forest.

'I just had this feeling we were at risk,' she finished, fully expecting Walter to pooh-pooh her fears.

Instead he sighed, a little sadly she thought. 'Ah yes, a rusky buzzy nest,' he agreed. 'The voi-voi-voice is tolling us, "Be war."'

'Beware?' Joe took him up. 'You mean you've managed to translate it? That forest noise?'

'Potty ... patty ... partly,' he admitted. 'A snuff to underspan a war-war-warning.'

'What about the creatures telling us to keep away?' Anna asked. 'Have you found out who they are?'

But on that issue he was far less certain, retreating into a mood of mystical vagueness. 'All wise one mi-mi-mind, the voi-voi-voice of good,' was all he would say, and he retreated further still, into an unwavering song that seemed strangely in keeping with the distant whine floating faintly across the water from the land.

It was those two sounds entwined – Walter's song

189

and the noise from the forest – which accompanied them during their slow journey along the coast. Lulled by it, Anna and Joe soon fell into an exhausted slumber, curled up together in the capsule; and that same weird harmony of voices was the first sound they heard when they awoke just before dawn.

By then they were flying only a rag of sail, just enough to keep them pointing into the wind.

'We reached the river mouth more than three hours ago,' Trog declared from his post at the tiller, while Og handed them an early morning meal with the words: 'There are no sleepy heads running this ship.'

'If you two are so wide awake,' Joe answered grumpily, accepting the proffered tray, 'what are we doing out here? We could be miles up river by now.'

'I have been advised to proceed with caution,' Trog explained evenly.

'Always better to look before you leap,' Og chipped in.

The reason for their caution became clear once the dawn broke – as did their need for a flat-bottomed boat – for stretched across the broad mouth of the river was a series of sandbars, with narrow channels in between. As the rising sun stained the sand a deep gold, they resumed their westward journey, weaving a path through the deepest of these channels.

Reliant only on sail, they made slow and difficult progress. One minute Og was trimming or backing the sails; the next he was up in the prow, sounding the depth of the water. But for all his care, still the flattened keel occasionally scraped the sand; and once they ran completely aground, the force of the current leaving them stranded on a gleaming sandbar.

That was the only time Walter took any notice of their situation. 'Oh dearly me,' he muttered, and drifted off into song once more.

Without any help from him, they all four heaved the boat back into the water and scrambled on board, resetting the sails before the tide could sweep them onto the opposite shore. Sand swirled in their wake, and then they were moving again, tacking this way and that as they negotiated the fine network of inter-linking channels.

There were far more signs of life out here than in the forest. Long-legged birds stalked the shallows; magnificent white-headed eagles perched watchfully on jutting pieces of driftwood; gulls, sandpipers, and other seabirds dotted the open stretches of sand; and glittering schools of fish veered away at their approach.

This was much more like the world Anna had read and heard about, the world she had witnessed through photographs and holograms in their training days on Titan. Harshness and death existed here – the sight of an eagle plucking a fish from the open water was proof enough of that – but so too did beauty and peace. The lazy flight of a gull, a cormorant airing its wings in the sun, a pair of otters cavorting in mid-stream, all demonstrated that this was a place where freedom and fear were held in balance. Only as the estuary fell behind them and they entered the main channel did Anna's sense of that balance begin to waver and fail.

Here, where the outer fringes of the forest struggled for survival in the sandy soil, there was more a feeling of threat. Fewer fish spangled the shallows; the birds, distrustful of the sunlight, preferred to skulk amongst the trees; and the occasional ground animal, emerging from the forest to drink, did so in the furtive manner of the hunted.

This brooding air of distrust only increased as they worked their way upstream. Now, with the banks lined by thick walls of green, a familiar hush had settled onto the forest. The distant hoot of a monkey or a parrot's grating cry was enough to make Boots flatten his ears and hiss at the empty sky. And as the boat tacked steadily from one side of the river to the other, Anna began to dread those few lingering seconds when they hovered close to the bank, deep in the shadow of the trees.

Yet for all her dread, there was no obvious sign of danger, no hint of anything monstrous lurking amongst the leaves. To the outward eye, all was as it should have been. Trog and Og went about their work unperturbed; Walter continued with his tone-less song; and the forest itself lay silent, even passive, beneath the mounting heat of the day.

By mid-afternoon the heat on the open deck had grown so intense that Trog steered the boat to the shady edge of the river where he and Og set about rigging up an awning with what remained of the insulation. While they worked, Joe clambered ashore, eager to inspect the forest at close quarters. Anna preferred to stay on board with Boots where she felt more secure.

It was while she was sitting in the prow, well away from the work going on, that she noticed the first of the crocodiles. She might easily have mistaken it for a floating log, but a slight movement of the tail revealed it for what it was. She made out the shape of the head then: the nostrils flared out as it filled its lungs for the next dive; the nobbled snout, more like a weathered piece of rock than part of a living thing;

and the eyes ...! They, more than anything else, caught her attention: one, a clear yellow colour; the other, dull white and sightless.

Blind? she thought curiously, and remembered the sharp claws of the bats on the island. Except there was no sign of bats here. So what else could have blinded something as powerful as a crocodile? And why did this one sink so cautiously beneath the surface, moving with the same furtive care as every other animal in the forest?

A much larger crocodile rose in the same spot, as if warned in advance that this was a safe place to surface, and again it was blind in one eye. Worse, its other eye had also been damaged. It occurred to her then that, with creatures as heavily armoured as these, the eyes were the most vulnerable part of the body. Given their long reptilian life, they stood more chance of being blinded than of anything else. Still the problem remained: what kind of animal would have the temerity to attack a crocodile?

She was still puzzling over this problem when she heard Joe calling from further along the bank.

Reluctantly, she stepped ashore and made for a tree that leaned out over the river. Joe was crouched at its base, inspecting a hole that burrowed down through the coiling roots.

'What do you think made a hole as big as this?' he asked, and was about to peer into it when she jerked him backwards.

'Don't get too near,' she warned him. 'There are crocs out on the river. This is probably where they hide.'

'Crocs? They don't live in holes. What have they got to hide from anyway? They're at the top of the food chain.'

'Not here they're not,' she said, and told him about the eyes of the crocs she had just seen.

She had barely finished when there was a noise directly behind them. She spun around, but it was only the tree creaking in the wind. Yet she could feel no wind on her cheek. The air was hot and still, the surface of the river unruffled. She peered up into the tangle of branches, and the tree moved again, one of its lower limbs bending a fraction as if borne downwards by some invisible weight. And all at once the pressure of the surrounding silence seemed to ease; the forest itself seemed to take a step backwards, leaving her room to move and breathe.

'Did you feel that?' she asked in a whisper.

Joe gazed at her blankly. 'Feel what?'

'That . . . that . . .' she began uncertainly, and was rescued by Trog, recalling them to the boat.

Back on the river they made slow progress. Shaded by the awning, they waited for each puff of wind, the sails bellying out for a few moments, then going slack again. Trog had fashioned a crude anchor from a scrap of metal, and at times they had to heave it overboard so as not to drift backwards. Marooned out there in the sluggish current, they became a part of the general stillness, with the forest pressing in on every side and unseen eyes observing them from the secret hollows of trunk and branch.

Not until the worst of the heat had passed did the breeze pick up. The first blast of cooler air came roaring through the treetops, ragged gusts chased each other across the river surface, and with a rattle of sails they lurched into motion.

'How far to go?' Anna shouted above the rush of wind and water. 'Can we get close to the transports before nightfall?'

'Distance too great to be completed in specified period,' Trog answered.

So, Anna thought, gazing at the sunlit scene before her, they would have to spend a night in the midst of the forest. For the present, with the boat dancing before the wind, that didn't seem a particularly daunting idea. On the other hand, she knew she would feel differently about it later. It had been precisely this – the prospect of enduring hours out here in the dark – which had sent her running back to Walter the day before. Yet was he really going to be of any help? He had hardly spoken since morning, totally engrossed in his wordless song. There were Trog and Og of course, but they wouldn't be much use against something like the bats. No, probably their best ally was the ship itself.

Casually, so as not to alarm Joe, she sauntered over and checked out the capsule. Like everything else on board it was looking the worse for wear. The once clear plastic cover was discoloured and beginning to craze; and the sleeping berth had become grubby and soiled from overuse. But at least the seals appeared to be intact.

She was about to close the cover, just to make sure, when Joe stepped up beside her.

'You're worried about tonight, aren't you?' he said quietly.

'A little.'

He pointed at the tangle of trees and vines that cloaked the bank. 'If we had to spend the night in there, unprotected, we'd probably have some problems. The big cats might prove to be a real hazard. But way out here . . .' He shook his head in disbelief. 'The chances are we're pretty safe. The crocs aren't likely to clamber on board; and even if they did, the transformers could handle them fairly easily.'

'It's not the crocs I'm worried about,' she admitted. 'It's the noise which starts up after dark.'

'But we don't even know what's causing it. Nor did the dolphins.'

'That's partly what bothers me.'

He shrugged vaguely. 'We can't afford to go looking for problems, Anna. Things are bad enough without that. Especially now Walter's gone crazy on us.'

'D'you really think he has?'

'Don't you? Listen to him. He's off with the fairies. We're on our own whether we like it or not. That's why we have to be practical. We have to face each challenge as it comes.'

'Isn't the forest one of those challenges?'

'Yes, but we're not actually in the forest,' he reminded her. 'Not yet anyway. Right now we're out on the water, the same as last night. What we have to concentrate on at this stage is getting up river. One thing at a time, Anna, otherwise we're finished.'

'So you're not worried . . .?' she began, but he cut across her.

'All right, I'm worried, it's true. Asleep, all I do is dream about the shark and the bats and all the other animals we've encountered so far. But those are real things. They're dangers we know about. They're not vague noises somewhere off in the dark. Like I said, we can't afford to fight a lot of imaginary battles on top of everything else.'

'Car nut ford to flight . . . fight atoll,' Walter murmured, breaking in upon their whispered discussion. 'Fighting car nut work year. Too money voi-voi-voices.'

Joe clicked his tongue impatiently. 'What are we

supposed to do if we don't fight? Just give up? Spend our time singing songs like you?'

'The hole whirl is sing-songing,' Walter replied. 'All wise the seam.' And he reverted to the low humming sound that had preoccupied him all day.

'You see,' Joe said. 'You can't put any store by what he says. He's as crazy as the rest of this planet. We'll go crazy too if we try and make sense of it. It's a madhouse, Anna, the sea-colonies saw to that. Our job is just to reach the transports and hold out for as long as we can. We're the first parents, remember. As I see it that's the one thing still worth fighting for.'

Anna didn't answer. Fighting! Did everything really come back to that in the end? To a war between them and the other intelligent species? If so, then what chance did they have? How could they possibly defeat the rest of creation?

Not for the first time she silently rejected Joe's view of things. Walter might be mad, but at least he was searching for another way. In a sense so was she. Because what she wanted above all was to understand. Knowledge is power, she had read once. If she could only solve the mystery behind the forest's silent threat, then perhaps ... perhaps ...

She turned inquiringly towards the forest itself, to where the sunlit day was already beginning to lose its lustre, the first hint of evening apparent in the shadows that reached across the river towards her. There was no ignoring those shadows, the night lurking like a live presence in the growing dark beneath the canopy.

'Whatever happens,' she said, glancing at Joe, 'sooner or later we have to come to terms with this place. Well, later may be good enough for you, but not for me. There's something out there, something scary, and I want to find out what it is.'

This time she didn't give him a chance to argue, but wandered off alone. He made no effort to follow, and she was glad of that, content to spend the remainder of the day perched in the prow with Boots; to watch the beauty of the river reveal itself as they wound their way ever deeper into the forest. Just be content with this, she kept telling herself – glorying in the blaze of a flowering vine or dazzled by the play of light on the water.

But as she had realised all along, the light could not last for ever. Gradually it lost its fierce intensity, the sun dropping towards the waiting canopy. Too soon, it seemed, the emerald glow of tree and vine deepened to the darker greens of evening; the surrounding air took on a dusky quality. For a few precious minutes the world stood poised between day and night. And in that brief interlude there was a flash of transparent wings as a dragonfly zoomed past Anna's head and hung motionless in the air before her.

It was exactly like her encounter beside the stream, when she had stepped from the forest and been confronted by a dragonfly's silent gaze. This creature, too, had red-tipped wings, and its multi-faceted eyes seemed fixed upon her.

Boots had stiffened in her arms, a ridge of fur standing up along his back. She tried to calm him, but with a growl he wriggled free and headed for the shelter of the capsule. Seconds later the dragonfly also disappeared as if its job were done, leaving her with the last of the sunlight.

Nervously she watched the sun's top edge vanish behind the trees. And in the sudden gloom the voice of the night began anew, even more shrill and insistent than she remembered. As if to accompany the sound, from the trees on either bank there arose a mist or smoke, which eddied and swirled on the fading breeze. At least smoke was what she took it for. Then, beneath the constant whine, she heard it – the rustle of countless wings – and all at once she understood.

The swarms!

The word the dolphins had used leaped into her mind unbidden, and she knew at last what it meant. She also knew, in the same instant, that the people in the dying sea-colonies had done the most terrible thing of all. Desperate, faced with an eternal dark, they had committed the unthinkable, seeding themselves not just upon the animals, but upon ... upon ...

Dimly, she was conscious of someone yelling at her, but for the moment she was too shocked to respond, unable to move until she felt the first sharp sting on her arm. It was that single jab of pain which finally broke through her astonishment and reminded her of the true peril they were in.

17

'Insects!' Joe was yelling. 'Millions of them!'

But by then Anna needed no warning. Already her head was encircled by a cloud of winged shapes, tiny feelers probing at her eyes, her ears, her nose. Half blinded, flapping her hands to keep them off, she staggered back along the deck to where Og waited calmly by the open capsule.

'The night is alive with the sound of insects,' he commented dryly, and clicked the lid shut behind her as she crawled in beside Joe and Boots.

Smarting from a dozen stings and bites, she gazed out through the plastic cover to where Trog and Og were standing together in the dusk. Although surrounded by the thickening swarm, they made no effort to cover their heads, the insects too small to damage their eyes. As if sensing that this was so, the swarm soon shifted the focus of its attack by descending on the capsule – pinging against the cover in their thousands.

'My God!' Joe burst out. 'Just look at them! You'd swear they were trying to force their way in.'

'No, they're too clever for that,' Anna said quietly.

He gave her a dazed, uncomprehending look. 'What?'

'See.' She pointed to where the insects had again

shifted the focus of their attack and were now clustered about the capsule's air intake. 'They've already worked out the best way of getting at us.'

She heard a slight sob as he drew in his breath. 'But that means . . .!'

She nodded. 'The people of the sea-colonies spliced their genes into everything that moved. *Everything!* Even these. They seeded the entire planet.'

'Oh come off it, Anna!' He drew away, as if trying to distance himself from the idea. 'No one could be that dumb.'

'I'd call it irresponsible, not dumb,' she corrected him, watching as Og scooped a layer of insects from the air intake only to have the swarm descend in greater numbers. 'The last colonies didn't have to worry about the future. They weren't going to be here. They thought they were free to transform the whole world; to turn every living thing into an image of themselves.'

'But thinking insects!' he protested. 'It sounds so far fetched.'

'Far fetched or not, it's the truth. Could insects carry on like this unless they had a mind? A *thinking* mind?'

Outside, the swarm had gathered so densely about Og's face that his one eye was completely obscured; and while he was temporarily blinded, a wedge of insects drove in through the tiny holes of the intake. There was a buzzing close beside Anna's ear and she just had time to reach out and close the inner seal. Several stray insects managed to spill through the inside vent, but Boots dispatched them with a few crunching bites. For the time being Anna and Joe were safe, but at a cost. They had cut off their air supply, which meant that in an hour or two they would suffocate.

'What are we going to do now?' Joe said, staring at her in consternation.

'There's Walter ...' she began, but Joe shook his head.

'Walter's no use. He didn't even sound the alarm.'

It was true. Either he had let them down or, worse, he had already been infested by the swarm.

'Walter!' she hissed urgently. 'Have they got to you yet?'

'Doughnut whirry,' he assured her, his voice unexpectedly calm. 'All is wall ... will ... well.'

Joe groaned and sank back onto the mattress. 'Here we are, with about a million insects trying to get at us, and all we have to rely on is an idiot.'

'There are such things as idiot savants,' Anna said hopefully. 'They're kind of wise fools.'

'Yeah, but Walter's not one of them. You've heard that song of his. He probably thinks he's an insect by now. He's not even on our side any more.'

'Nut so,' Walter interrupted softly, his voice only fractionally louder than the shrill buzz seeping in from the outer night. 'Only won seed ... side fur avery biddy. The humus side. All critters are won and the seam. All are dozens.'

'We're all what?'

'Cous-cous-cousins.'

'Cousins!' Joe exclaimed. 'To those six-legged things out there? You must be off your head!'

'Hush!' Anna advised him, taking her cue from Boots who had begun to growl uneasily. 'Something's going on.'

It was now too dark to see outside, and they all fell silent, listening. For what? At first Anna could hear only the high-pitched cry of the swarm. Then, beneath the muffled din of the night, she detected another sound – more of a scratching than anything else, and curiously persistent, as though tiny claws or mandibles were working at a tough, resistant surface.

'What is it?' Joe breathed, but Anna, with a cold feeling of dread, had already guessed.

'They're trying to chew through the seals.'

The fear in Joe's voice was unmistakable. 'D'you think they can?'

She had to struggle to stave off panic. 'It depends how tough the seals are.'

'But we can't just wait and see! What about the transformers? Can't they clear around the seals?'

'Not inside the air vent they can't, and that's where most of the scratching's coming from.'

'Well, we have to do *something!*' he said desperately.

She had no argument with that. Yet what options did they still have? Clearly they were trapped – surrounded by forest and with the dawn still eight or more hours away. There was simply nowhere to hide. No possible refuge.

Unless . . .!

It occurred to her then that the forest animals managed to survive in spite of everything. The crocs by burrowing in amongst the tree roots; the birds by hollowing out trunks and branches. So why didn't the insects force their way into *those* hiding places? What was it that kept the animals safe? There had to be a reason, a common factor, something to explain their survival.

As she lay there racking her brains, her whole body damp with fear, the answer came to her. Yes, of course! The trees! They were the common factor. Every animal in the forest had found a way of nesting within the trees themselves. In some inexplicable way the trees protected them. Perhaps their leaves put out some kind of repellant chemical; their bark or foliage might even have been poisonous. But for whatever reason the trees were the answer. Or so she dearly hoped.

'Walter?' she whispered, her voice steadier now. 'Are you still there?'

'Steel year,' he responded placidly.

'Is there enough breeze to get us to shore?'

'A snuff.'

'Then listen to me carefully. I want Trog to steer over to the bank and to tie up under the first big tree he comes to. Right underneath it, do you understand?'

'Udder stand,' he replied, and the craft heeled slightly as it changed course.

While they were making for the shore, Anna explained her idea to Joe. 'It's our only chance,' she finished. 'If this doesn't work . . .'

'Let's not think about that yet,' he cut in hastily, and reached for her hand.

Clinging to each other in the dark, they heard the craft scrape against the reed-lined bank and come to rest. There was a clatter of footsteps from out on the deck as Og tied up, a murmured 'Miss urn encompassed' from Walter, and after that just the continued whine of the insects.

For a while nothing more happened, Anna listening so hard that she failed to notice how Boots had stopped growling. It wasn't until he began to purr that she truly allowed herself to relax.

'I think it's working,' Joe whispered excitedly.

Sure enough, a minute or two later the scratching noise stopped altogether and the whine of insect voices seemed to recede. They were replaced by a much gentler sound.

Neither she nor Joe understood what was happening – the night too dark for that, especially there under the tree – but they soon took heart from the profound sense of peace which settled about the craft. Cautiously they opened the air vent, just a fraction at first, and then wider as nothing more terrible than the musty scents of the night flowed in.

'Eat a cock and all swill,' Walter droned contentedly, and again began to sing, though now his song was anything but insect-like and toneless. To Anna's ear it was filled with creaks and swishing noises that might easily have arisen from the living heart of the forest, so natural did they seem.

Now what did *this* song remind her of? she wondered as she snuggled against Joe. But after their recent ordeal she was too tired to think clearly, soon drifting off to sleep where she dreamed that someone – who? – was serenading the assorted trees and bushes that clustered along the river's edge.

★   ★   ★

She awoke to a greenish light and to the chill touch of early morning. Rolling over she felt for Joe, but he was gone, the lid of the capsule thrown open.

'Anna?' she heard him whisper from outside. 'I want you to see this.'

Still half asleep she crawled out onto the deck, which seemed at first glance to be enclosed by a shimmering wall – a wall that filtered the dawn light and stained everything the same soft shade of green. She blinked and looked again and realised that they were surrounded by leafy branches which had dipped down during the night, shutting the craft off from the threatening dark.

205

She had hardly taken this in when those same branches began to stir in response to the coming day. With a series of creaks and groans they lifted clear of the deck, swinging slowly upwards and allowing the early sunlight to flood through. Dazzled by it, she gazed wonderingly at the tree's massive trunk as if expecting it to speak to her; but it remained as stolid and voiceless as ever, the overarching branches moving languidly in the gathering breeze.

'The trees close up at night!' Joe murmured, as astonished as she. 'Which means they're either light-sensitive or . . . or . . .'

'I think there's more to it than that,' she suggested softly, and saw with relief that Joe too had guessed the dark truth.

'I could hardly believe it when I first came out here,' he confessed in an awed whisper, 'but it's the only explanation there is. The only convincing one anyway. The trees – these big ones – they can *think*.'

She nodded in solemn agreement. 'They're the same as everything else. The people of the sea-colonies spliced human genes into them as well. Their last act was to leave the whole planet partly human.'

'Connect,' Walter responded in the background, and let out a babble of such childlike laughter that Anna was transported back to those first few hours after landing, when everything had seemed much less complicated.

'What's there to be so happy about?' she asked.

'Ivory buddy is humus,' he crowed in delight. 'Allah dozens. Allah won beg fumbly.'

'What was that?'

'We're all cousins,' Trog translated. 'We're all one big family.'

'Brothers and sisters of the world unite,' Og added, and clamped a metal hand around the nearest branch.

'Families don't always get on together,' Anna reminded them. 'And that includes brothers and sisters. Sometimes they fight more than strangers.'

'Nut wan they torque,' Walter countered, still laughing. 'Nut wan they community gate.'

'How can they talk when they don't share a single language?' she argued in turn. 'When they have no way of understanding each other?'

That chastened him, as she had guessed it might, and again he retreated into his toneless song.

'You're wasting your time,' Joe whispered. 'He's suffered too much damage to think straight. Not that it matters any more. We can look after ourselves now. Last night proves that.'

'Correction,' Trog broke in. 'You are currently in the care of the ship, its personnel, and, I am informed, the tree under which we now shelter, botanical name unknown.'

'The tree of life, we presume,' Og joined in quietly, and set about casting off.

'You can call it what you like,' Joe replied, facing defiantly into the breeze as they set sail once again, 'but it saved us, that's all I care about. It proved we can survive here without Walter's help.'

Could they? Anna wondered, and gazed with fresh eyes at the surrounding forest. Could they really do without Walter's help altogether? Or was Joe being over-optimistic?

As the river uncoiled beneath them, she secretly directed that same question to the trees slipping past on either bank. But no matter how hard she tried, she could imagine no answer that made any sense,

207

the forest as silent and still as the sunlight. Apart from the gurgle of water along the ship's sides and the occasional chattering cry from amongst the trees, Walter's was the only voice that disturbed the morning, both then and later, the drone of his song continuing tirelessly.

'I wish he'd shut up,' Joe said at one point. 'That insect noise of his gives me the creeps.'

Anna also found it unsettling. Yet when it stopped abruptly in mid-afternoon, allowing the silence to deepen eerily about them, she almost wished he would go on.

'What's up now, Walter?' she demanded, for they were cruising towards a sandy spit that thrust out from the bank.

'Earned of jenny ... johnny ... journey,' he announced.

'You mean the transports are here?' she asked excitedly, she and Joe scanning the snarl of vines and trees on the nearby shore.

'Nut year egg slackly,' he corrected her. 'Land in sight loc-loc-located sexy kilo matters to the naughty weasel.'

'Where?'

'He says the transports are six kilometres to the north-west,' Trog explained, swinging the tiller hard and using the speed of the craft to drive it onto the outjutting spit.

With a grating sound they juddered to a halt, and Trog and Og immediately began clearing the decks, hurling sections of dismantled keel down onto the sand. Og leaped after them, one hand transformed into a cutting device for shearing away the outriggers.

'What's the plan now then?' Anna asked, comforting Boots who was spooked by all the commotion.

'We have been instructed to convert the ship into a land vehicle,' Trog replied, and positioned himself under one of the heavy engines which was about to break free.

'London bridge is falling down,' Og warned them, and snipped through the last strut, the sudden weight of the engine driving Trog's splayed feet deep into the sand.

With no visible effort, he lowered it to the ground and trotted around to the other side where Og was already busy.

'So how long is this conversion going to take?' Anna cried, having to raise her voice above the noise of the work.

'Difficult to estimate with exactitude,' Trog answered.

'How long roughly?' Joe insisted.

'Between twelve and twenty-four hours,' Trog chirruped, grappling with the second engine; while Og added breezily: 'Unlike Rome, this will be built in a day.'

'A whole day!' Joe protested. 'We could walk to the transports faster than that. They're only six kilometres away after all.'

It was what Anna had been dreading, and she glanced uncertainly at the backdrop of the forest.

'Well, what do you think?' Joe said, looking straight at her. 'With Trog to guide us, we'd easily get there before dark, if that's what's worrying you.'

Yet it wasn't just the dark that made her hesitate. The forest itself was what she shrank from. After their last abortive expedition she had no desire to re-enter its green-tinged gloom, to share its shadowy spaces with the hidden swarms. And there was something else: despite all that they had said about

Walter – how he was crazed and damaged beyond repair – she was loath to leave without him. For all his faults he had brought them this far, and some instinct warned her that it would be foolish to desert him now.

'What do *you* say, Walter?' she asked, appealing directly to him. 'Should we take Trog and go on ahead?'

But he failed to respond.

'Walter is not to be disturbed,' Trog intoned from below. 'I am informed that he is fully occupied with the task of translating the insect language.'

'And if it isn't a language?' Joe objected. 'If it turns out to be a lot of noise?'

'The likelihood of such an outcome not yet computed,' Trog confessed.

And Og: 'The jury's still out on that one.'

Joe turned to Anna, more determined than she had seen him in days. 'Well, you can please yourself, but I'm not waiting around here. Walter can waste his own time. I've got a job to do. So, are you coming or staying?'

She cast another nervous glance towards the brooding face of the forest, as hesitant as before. 'If we could just . . . just wait a while,' she began, but Joe, having lost patience, was already clambering over the side.

'Come on, Trog,' she heard him say, 'I need you to clear a path.'

'Walter has instructed me . . .' Trog began, but Joe was as short with him as he had been with Anna.

'Correct me if I'm wrong,' he barked out, 'but I thought the protection of human personnel was your primary directive.'

'I am also a person according to Walter,' Trog

muttered audibly, but he followed Joe just the same.

'Birds of a feather flock together,' Og called after them.

And it was that cry, as much as the sight of Joe making doggedly for the trees, which decided Anna. Regardless of what her instincts told her, she could not allow him to go off alone. Not at this stage. If she had to part company with anyone, then sadly it would have to be with Walter.

'Wait for me!' she called, and having stowed Boots in the capsule so he wouldn't be tempted to follow, she slipped over the side and ran to catch up.

It was a comfort to have Joe's hand in hers when they stepped together into the forest. Even so, there was no ignoring the chill she felt as the canopy closed over them; nor the sense that this, the final stage of their journey, could lead only to disaster.

18

The afternoon was well advanced when they neared their destination, long looping shadows already hanging beneath the trees. In that gloomy atmosphere they came upon the landing site – a whole hillside shorn of forest, with just a few burned-out stumps remaining. Littered untidily amongst these stumps were the hulking shapes of the transports: some half-buried in a tangle of fire-blackened undergrowth; others lying on their sides in the open, their once gleaming panels now torn or stained by earth and smoke.

'Dear God!' Joe breathed, and sat down with a bump.

Anna, unable to speak for the moment, could only look on miserably. It was as if that vague sense of doom which had stalked her throughout the afternoon had at last taken visible form. Here before her, in the shattered remains of the transports, was the end of all those dreams which had begun two years before on Titan.

'They were supposed to land gently!' Joe burst out, struggling to hold back tears. 'They had sensors on board, to pick out clear landing sites.'

'Initial evidence suggests that sensors were damaged on entry,' Trog declared. 'High probability that electronic heat shields failed on all craft, including our own. Design fault is most likely cause.'

'That'll do, Trog,' Anna said, cutting him short. 'You can make a full inspection tomorrow. I've seen enough for one day. Now let's get back to Walter.'

She was already turning away in disappointment when Trog's hand clamped upon her shoulder.

'It should be noted that the sun will set in seventeen minutes,' he intoned. 'Insufficient time to return before nightfall. Imperative that you find shelter in close vicinity.'

Only seventeen minutes until sunset! Anna had been so taken up with this scene of devastation that she hadn't given a thought to their immediate safety. Now, for the first time, she looked at the lengthening shadows and shivered. As if to emphasise her fear a dragonfly appeared, hovering close to her face for a second or two, its eyes glittering dangerously.

'We have to get out of here,' she whispered as it sped away.

Joe had risen cautiously to his feet. 'There was a big tree back there,' he murmured.

But she was already shaking her head. 'The tree on its own won't give us enough shelter. We'll need some kind of hiding place as well, the same as the other animals – the same as last night when we stayed in the capsule. I'd say our best bet for tonight is to look for a sealed compartment in one of the transports.'

'And if there isn't one? They seem in pretty bad shape to me.'

'Let's see,' she replied, and made for the nearest vessel.

It was amongst the biggest of the transports, loaded with supplies and designed to double as living quarters in the years ahead. Not that anyone would ever live in it now. Under impact its nose had crumpled, its inner frame had twisted and collapsed, and a jagged gash had opened along the length of its hull.

Anna approached that opening now, but on the point of climbing inside, she paused. Something about the inner darkness deterred her. Was that a faint stirring she could detect? The wind sounding through the hull perhaps?

She was standing there undecided when Trog hissed a warning in her ear.

'Do not enter. I repeat, do not enter. Ship infested by the swarm.'

She backed off hastily, her flesh creeping at the thought of what might have happened had she climbed into the dark interior.

'Watch out!' she called, seeing Joe approach another of the hulks. 'Let Trog check it for you first.'

That ship also proved to be infested, as did the next four they tried.

By then the forest floor had grown distinctly gloomy, even there where fire had cleared a path.

'Six minutes to sunset,' Trog reported, clambering through the blackened undergrowth in their wake. 'Shelter now a triple-A priority.'

Anna turned on him angrily. 'D'you think we don't know that already?' she yelled, and immediately regretted her outburst as the surrounding forest seemed to rustle in response.

Taking several deep breaths, she fought down her panic and forced herself to assess the situation. Over to her right Joe was backing off from yet another of the ruined ships, his eyes fixed warily on the gaping hole in its side. So what now? With the minutes slipping rapidly by, they had no hope of checking the whole fleet. It was spread over too wide an area. In any case, what was the use? So far every ship had been infested, and there was no reason to believe the rest would be any different. What they needed was an undamaged craft, or at least one that hadn't been holed – though even if such a ship existed, there was still the problem of how to locate it.

She swung around as the answer came to her.

'Trog!' she rapped out. 'Scan the area for electronic activity!'

'Scanning now,' he intoned, and his head began to swivel, moving from a northerly direction round towards the west and then the south where it suddenly locked into position, his one eye glowing in the descending dusk.

'Impulses proceeding from a source located approximately three hundred metres . . .' he began, pointing down the slope, but she didn't wait for the rest.

'This way!' she yelled to Joe, and set off at a run.

Above her the canopy was gilded with a mere skim of sunlight, which was all that remained of the day. At any moment, as she knew full well, those last rays could blink out. And after that! She cast a terrified glance at the sombre shape of a hulk as she hurried past, imagining what lurked within.

'Two minutes remaining,' Trog called after her, as if divining her fear.

Two minutes! She was aware of Joe racing along behind, his body crashing through the burned remnants of the undergrowth. Fending off the blackened twigs and branches that whipped at her as she ran, she searched the shadowy bottom of the slope, her eyes straining against the gloom. And glimpsed

215

something! A flash of silver, that was all, but it was enough.

'There!' she sang out, and increased her pace, half falling down the last and steepest portion of the slope and landing on her knees in the soft mud bordering a stream.

The ship, much smaller than most, was nestled in the stream bed near the opposite bank, and with Joe beside her she splashed towards it.

'Where's the airlock?' she gasped, the pair of them groping frantically along the ship's undamaged sides.

Before they could find it the sun dipped below the horizon and the night was upon them. Instantly a thin whine of insect voices filled the surrounding space. But there was another sound too – a series of splashing footsteps – and Trog was there at their side, his arm telescoping outwards as he reached for the emergency lever.

A door slid open just above head height, a greenish light spilling out, and with the first of the insects bombarding them they scrambled up and through the opening, into the airlock itself.

Bitten and stung, their faces buried in their arms, they were in no state to secure the ship; but again Trog was there to help, closing the door with one hand while with the other he plucked the remaining insects from the air.

'You have boarded craft number BU03,' he declared evenly, and punched the lever that controlled the inner door.

Anna, still struggling to regain her breath, took in the number of the craft without really registering what it meant. Only when the inner door slid back and she felt the icy breath of the ship's interior did the full significance of that number strike home.

'BU03!' she exclaimed. 'That means this is a breeding unit, one of the three incubator ships!'

Together they entered the main storage cabin – a long, low-ceilinged room lit by the same greenish light as the airlock and with banks of clear plastic containers lining the walls. It was freezing cold, a glittering sheen of frost covering everything; but even through the frost there was no mistaking the baby shapes that huddled within each of the containers. Anna scraped a hand across the nearest plastic surface, revealing the mute face of an unborn child, its eyes closed as if in sleep.

'They've survived the landing!' she breathed excitedly, a cloud of vapour billowing from her mouth, out into the stillness of the room. 'They're just waiting to be revived. To be born!'

She turned towards Joe, expecting him to share her excitement, but all he did was shrug uncomfortably.

'Maybe they're better off as they are,' he muttered, and indicated the confined space of the cabin. 'We couldn't rear them in here – we'd end up as crazy as Walter – and the living-quarters have been taken over by the swarms. That leaves only the forest. We could build some kind of shelter, I suppose, something to protect them by day, but at night ...' He shrugged again, his voice trailing off into the silence.

For some minutes Anna was too busy coping with her own disappointment to make any reply.

'So what do we do?' she said at last. 'Leave them as they are? Never revive them?'

'That might be the kindest way.'

She couldn't help herself then, all the stored frustration of recent days bursting out of her. 'You mean we've made this whole journey for nothing? You want us to give up? To hide away here until we're too old to fend for ourselves? While all the time these children . . . these children . . .'

But the many unborn faces, dimly visible within their frosted plastic containers, were too much for her, and smearing the tears from her eyes she ran the length of the ship and entered the forward cabin.

It was much warmer in there, the furthermost wall covered with rows of lights and flickering dials. As Joe and Trog entered behind her, a screen flashed on and several lines of print appeared along the top. The message read:

> We know this ship has survived. What is happening? Vital that you make contact as soon as possible.
> Project must go ahead. We repeat: project must go ahead.

Joe looked across at her. 'What should we tell them?'

'Don't ask me,' she said, feeling suddenly defeated.

He moved towards the transmitter. 'How about just saying we're safe?'

'Safe!' She gave an unhappy laugh. 'With a million insects trying to get at us?'

'You know what I mean.' He shuffled his feet awkwardly. 'We could at least put their minds at rest. Let them know we're still alive.'

She brushed the hair wearily from her face. 'What's the use? They'll only start asking questions. Or worse, give us instructions we daren't carry out.'

He made a small helpless gesture. 'What then?'

She thought for a minute or two. 'Another few

hours of waiting won't hurt them,' she said finally, and slumped into the nearest chair. 'Right now all I want is to sleep. Things may look better in the morning.'

Yet she knew the reverse might well be true. If anything, the clear light of day would only reveal their plight more starkly. Because the simple facts were unavoidable: she and Joe could not abandon the children waiting there in the frozen compartment, and neither, in all fairness, could they revive them. Birth was a promise of life to come, and what kind of life could growing children expect in the heart of this forest, ruled as it was by the insect armies of the night? No, it would be a base and miserable form of existence, unworthy of them.

What then? she asked herself, echoing Joe's earlier question. There was no possibility of moving the children to a safer place. If she had learned one thing from their journey, it was that nowhere was really safe. Not on this transformed version of the planet Earth where human guile and cunning had taken on monstrous shape.

Yes, *human guile and cunning*, that was what they were up against. And human kindness? Human compassion? What had happened to those qualities? Had they somehow fled the world? Had they been lost – left out perhaps – when the human genes governing intelligence were spliced into the rest of creation? Had the last colonies passed on only the very worst of themselves, donating to the other species only their aggression and their drive for dominance? Was this the truth behind the one mind, the one voice, Walter had referred to? It was a horrible thought which she flinched away from. A world without love! Without gentleness or care or fellow feeling! She could not bring herself to face such a prospect. Not at that moment. Not at the end of a long exhausting day.

Tomorrow, she decided wearily, sinking back into the chair and closing her eyes against this, the most hateful evening of her life. Tomorrow would be soon enough. She would deal with it all then.

★   ★   ★

She thought she was still dreaming when she heard the song, a high trilling melody made up of two voices twined together. There was so much happiness in those voices that she knew they could not be real; they had to be a part of some dream existence where hope and gaiety still held sway.

With that thought she opened her eyes onto the real world. Yet astonishingly the song continued, coming from somewhere beyond the ship and growing ever louder.

Joe slept on beside her, and careful not to disturb him, she tiptoed over to the windscreen and rubbed a clear space in the fogged glass. Outside, the forest lay draped in early morning mist, the sunlight struggling to break through. There was no breeze, and in the ghostly stillness the voices reached her with unnatural clarity. One she recognised straight away as Walter's. The other, it seemed, was Og's, surprisingly full-throated and enthusiastic, as if he shared Walter's obvious delight in this new day. Though what there was for either of them to be so pleased about, Anna had no idea.

A much smaller airlock had been installed there in the cabin, and she activated it now, the swish of the inner door rousing Joe.

220

'Wha's up?' he asked thickly.

'Walter's arrival is imminent,' Trog answered for her. 'He brings, I am told, news of some import.'

'Fat chance of that,' Joe muttered, unimpressed, and stood up stiffly.

Although it was a tight fit, they all three managed to squeeze into the airlock, which opened to a cool crisp morning. The first stirrings of a breeze tugged gently at the mist, and the nearby stream bubbled and chattered to itself as if full of stifled laughter. But above all it was Walter and Og's song which dominated the forest's deeper silence – that and a strange chugging noise which never varied.

'What the hell's that?' Joe wondered aloud, peering into the mist.

And in a sudden shaft of sunlight they saw Walter. He was trundling along the bed of the stream towards them – no longer a sea-going craft, but a weird-looking land vehicle. Gone were the stern rudder, the masts, the sails. The two engines, formerly used as outriggers, had been mounted crosswise beneath the hull, more like giant axles than anything else; and attached to either end of each engine were crude caterpillar-style wheels fashioned from scraps of unused metal.

'Gruntings from the purple to the purple,' Walter sang out.

'He means greetings,' Trog explained unnecessarily.

And Og, from his post high on the deck: 'We bring you glad tidings of great joy.'

With a final rumble from the engines, the craft lurched to a halt in the shallow water of the stream; and Boots, mewing a welcome, leaped down into Anna's waiting arms.

221

'Hairy is, purple none bar six,' Walter cried as Anna rubbed her cheek against the misty dampness of Boots' fur.

'He's not people, Walter,' Joe pointed out quietly. 'Nor are you. It's about time you got that straight.'

'Thus were your rung . . . rang . . . wrong,' Walter replied, unabashed. 'Purple everyworm.'

'Everywhere?' Anna took him up, and waded into the stream towards him, the water striking cold on her bare legs. 'If you're talking about the insects, they came close to getting us last night.' She pointed at the ruined ships strewn across the burned-out slope above them. 'They've taken over all the transports bar one. The project's finished. They'd have finished us too if it hadn't been for this breeding unit, and that's no good without the rest. Thanks to your so-called people there's nothing for us here.'

Walter let out a peal of carefree laughter. 'Rung agin,' he countered. 'One brooding you knit is allah we needle. Jest live the rust to yours trilly.'

'You mean you can take care of the insects for us?' Joe asked, his voice heavy with distrust.

'Izzy as pee. Dud nut I till you? All wise one mine. One voi-voi-voice. The voi-voi-voice of good.'

'Those are empty words, Walter,' Anna objected. 'They may make you feel better, but they don't change anything. The swarms haven't gone away; they'll still kill us given the chance.'

Walter chugged into motion, rumbling forward until his prow was almost touching her breast. 'No, nut jest humpty worms,' he disagreed, speaking with a new intensity now, the bubble of laughter still there in his voice, but subdued. 'Lust note . . . night, I beckon to under stunned.'

'You began to understand what?'

'The lung witch of the swim . . . swam . . . swarms. I listed to thumb, to wattle they were sighing.'

'You can translate their language?' Joe asked, no more trusting than before. 'Understand what they're saying?'

'Bet your life he can,' Og cut in.

'They spike of the Quins' Parlances, dip in the furriest,' Walter continued. 'The police war the Quins held cut an muck the lawns for allah the purple of . . .'

'Hold on, Walter,' Anna interrupted. 'We're not following this. You'll have to go more slowly.'

'Butter stall,' he suggested. 'Oval to Trig and Ug.'

'Walter's account is as follows,' Trog began dutifully. 'The swarms spoke of something called the Queens' Palaces, located deep in the forest. It is where all laws governing the swarms are enacted, and it is in Walter's opinion the seat of power.'

'It's where the action is,' Og added.

'What Walter is proposing,' Trog went on, 'is that we go in search of these Palaces in order to put our case.'

'What case is that?' Joe asked.

'We explain to them our common heritage. It is Walter's view that once they understand the kinship which binds us all, they will cease to oppose our project.'

'We'll be one big happy family,' Og came in again.

And from Walter: 'One mine car nut warn agates hits elf.'

'Who says so?' Joe challenged him. 'There was no shortage of wars in the old days, even amongst people of the same race.'

'That is mutually agreed,' Trog answered on Walter's behalf. 'But such warring groups were not of

223

one mind. They had ceased to speak a common language or to share common goals. Communication had broken down. The result was conflict. Walter's plan is to prevent such conflict by going in search of the Queens' Palaces. Now that he understands the insect language, he is in a position to plead with those who govern the swarms. He is inviting you to accompany him.'

'You've got a ticket to ride,' Og put in.

'Hip a bard . . . a beard . . . aboard,' Walter suggested with an eager laugh. And when Joe and Anna didn't move. 'Wattle are you whiting fur?'

'Well, you can count me out for one,' Joe said firmly, his mind clearly made up. 'I've heard enough of your crazy ideas, Walter. At least we're safe here. That's more than we'll be if we follow you into the middle of nowhere.'

Walter's laughter was replaced by a sigh. 'End you, An . . . An . . . Anna? Are you stying bee hive . . . behave . . . behind as swill? Err are you combing a ling . . . lung . . .long?'

She very nearly refused him point blank, like Joe. But then she looked at his patched and battered hull, at his damaged engines and makeshift metal wheels, and in spite of all that she saw, still she was tempted to go with him. For better or worse this beaten-up wreck *was* Walter; and she had lived with him for too long, grown too used to his weird ways of thinking and speaking, to give him up without a struggle.

'I'm not sure,' she confessed unhappily.

'Not sure!' Joe was staring at her in astonishment. 'But he doesn't know where these Palaces are or whether they really exist. He may wander around out there until he breaks down for good. Just look at him, at the state he's in! He can't go on for ever. Even if

224

he finds the Palaces, so what? Do you honestly believe that the swarm Queens will listen to him? That the insects will agree to treat us differently from every other animal in the forest just because we share some common genes?'

'One mine,' Walter murmured in the background, as if sensing her hesitation. 'Nut jest junes.'

And Og, driving the point home: 'Great minds think alike.'

'There's one other thing,' Joe went on, ignoring them both. 'If he reaches the Palaces, he'll be in the heart of enemy territory, the most dangerous place in the whole forest. If you're there with him, what chance will you have of getting out alive? They'll overwhelm you, and none of Walter's crazy talk will be able to stop them.'

'He did manage to bring us this far,' she pointed out, glancing from Walter to Joe.

'Yes, and this is where we should stay. It's where we're meant to be. All those unborn children in there are relying on us. Without us, they don't have a hope. Are you prepared just to walk out and leave them?'

'But last night you said there was nothing else for us to do!' she protested, caught in an agony of indecision. 'You said leaving them might be the kindest way.'

'Well, I've thought better of it since and I've changed my mind. Walking out would be the worst kind of betrayal. Also, there's nowhere to go. The whole planet's contaminated. This is probably as good a place as any. If we stay, who knows? With Trog's help we can try and build some form of shelter. Start a small colony. That'll be something, Anna, and we won't have those children in there on our conscience.'

It was his last argument which swayed her; and in a quick parting gesture she reached up and brushed her hand against Walter's dented prow.

'I'm sorry, Walter,' she murmured sadly. 'Joe's right. Our place is here.'

She was expecting another of his disappointed sighs, but instead – as if to say, this is how things should be – he gave a reassuring chuckle which spread through the surrounding forest like warm sunlight.

'Nothing like a good laugh,' Og commented, and promptly joined in.

As their laughter died away, there was a rumble from the engines and Anna stepped back.

'Wash me lurk . . . lick . . . luck,' Walter declared, trundling slowly forward.

Anna tried, but by then she was too upset to say a word. Clutching Boots, she watched through misty eyes as Walter and Og clattered off down the stream, his wheels throwing up a spray of mud and weed.

Just before they disappeared from view, Walter called out encouragingly: 'Nut to fee . . . foe . . . fear, Fran-Fran-Frankie's year.'

'Frankie?' Joe asked, giving Anna a puzzled look.

It was Og who answered. 'St Francis to the rescue!' he cried, his toneless robot voice floating back through the trees.

19

Everything seemed to go flat after Walter left, for Anna especially. Although she and Joe rarely spoke of him, it was more or less understood that he would never return, and that knowledge cast a shadow over her days. The forest at large, which had once impressed her with its beauty, now appeared drab and uninteresting, hardly less resplendent than the burned-out section of hillside fronting their new home. Even the giant trees, which rustled in sympathy whenever she passed, became hardly more than a backdrop to her humdrum existence.

The change, as she was fully aware, lay in herself, not in the forest. Yet seemingly there was nothing she could do to improve her plight. She would wake up feeling listless and lost, wondering how to fill the long hours ahead; and at unexpected moments throughout the day she would find herself on the verge of tears, usually for little or no reason.

Again and again she asked herself the question: was it Walter himself she missed or was it just the childlike joy that he brought with him? But she could never decide. She knew only that her present life, there in the prison-like confines of the valley, was intolerable.

To his credit, Joe did all he could to cheer her up,

involving her in everything; and she in turn did her best to join in, though as often as not she felt more of a hindrance than a help.

Their overall survival plan was simple: to get Trog to dismantle parts of the ruined transports and to use those materials in the construction of a new shelter. They started work that very first day, with Anna marking out the ground plan beside the stream while Joe supervised Trog further up the slope. By evening they had made some progress, the beginnings of a barnlike structure already taking shape. By the following morning, however, their new building had become just another nesting site for the swarm, which buzzed irritably if anyone ventured near.

Undeterred, they started again, except this time they constructed the shelter in closed sections which they intended opening up later, when the building as a whole was complete. But again the swarm outwitted them, by using burrowing insects to dig their way up from below.

Their third effort, which included a solid metal base, met with initial success. After ten hours of bruising labour the first fully enclosed compartment stood gleaming on the forest floor.

'Let's see what the swarm can do about *that*,' Joe said as they walked back to the ship in the evening light – the onset of dusk, as always, accompanied by the watchful presence of a dragonfly.

The next morning it looked as though they had at last hit on the right answer, for their new building was untouched. But once again the swarm had merely changed tactics. No sooner had they started work on a second compartment than clouds of sand-flies and mosquitoes descended on the valley, driving them back to the ship; and that night, for the first time, the ship itself came under attack, with insects swarming all over it.

Up until then they had agreed neither to activate the incubators nor to contact Titan. While their future remained so uncertain, it seemed unfair to bring children into the world. Similarly, they could see no point in sending false messages of hope. It was better to wait and to contact the authorities only when they had something positive to transmit. Yet with the ship under nightly siege and their future less certain than ever, they began to rethink their position. In their hearts they both felt that perhaps the only message they could possibly send would be a warning, a caution to the people of Titan to stay clear of Earth for ever.

Because it was now difficult for them to go outside, Trog had to work largely alone. As a result the progress on the building slowed.

Hampered by clouds of midges which made it difficult for him to see, Trog frequently failed to close off the next section before nightfall, and soon more than half the new shelter was infested. The nights, meanwhile, were even more depressing, with the ship under attack from dusk till sunrise.

Waking in the small hours, Anna would clear the fog from the windscreen and see nothing but a mass of squirming bodies, the rasp of their legs and wings sending an uneasy murmur through the ship. That murmur told her something she had sensed from the moment of Walter and Og's departure: that she and Joe could not hold out for ever. Eventually the ship would be breached.

Sure enough, one night she was roused by a furtive rustling in the wall. 'Joe!' she whispered, nudging him awake. 'They're inside the hull.'

'What?' He sat up in the dark. 'They can't be.'

But they were. Somehow, through some chink or crevice even Trog was unable to detect, they had found a way in.

'Insects are currently exploring the ventilation system,' Trog intoned, staring unblinkingly at them in the dark. 'I suggest prompt action before they damage the circuitry and affect the ship's basic functions. Should that happen, the incubators would be put at risk.'

That was all the warning Anna needed. With Joe's help she tore the cover from the nearest vent and coaxed Boots in through the hole. It was a task he had shown himself expert at once before, weeks earlier, back at the oasis. Letting out a single growl he was gone, the swish of his body along the network of pipes punctuated by the sound of hard-shelled bodies breaking apart.

Ever quick to learn, Boots was the one who woke them on the following night, his sharp ears picking up the first faint noises from the vent. And from then on it was his nightly patrols that kept them safe, though always it took him a little longer to clear the hull; and always, when he emerged, he looked a little more bedraggled.

In an attempt to give the ship more protection, they had Trog tow it along the stream to the cover of a giant tree. It was a decision they soon regretted. At twilight the tree duly enclosed them with its boughs; but by dawn, all the leaves had been stripped away and the tree was as good as dead. Clearly, even the trees' mysterious defences broke down under the combined assault of the gathering swarms.

After that the attacks grew in intensity, the scrabble of insect bodies keeping them awake for hours on end. Joe, enraged by his own powerlessness, took to prowling about the ship until well after midnight. Sometimes, lying alone in the dark, Anna would hear him beating his fist against the hull in frustration, and she would wonder, with scant hope, whether Walter had managed to reach the Palaces and plead their cause to the Queens.

Unlike Joe, she endured the siege with a curious detachment. It was as if she had all but lost the will to survive; as if she had known all along that the planet would destroy them eventually. And with that realisation came a false calm. Nothing seemed to matter any more, not the threat of death, nor even the loss of those dreams she had brought with her from Titan. Trapped within the ship, she spent hours gazing at the tiny baby faces in their glittering plastic containers, vaguely relieved that they had never known the gift of life only to have it snatched away; that they would never experience this feeling of emptiness which had come to blight her own existence.

Listless, adrift in a sea of uncaring, she came to regard the last half hour before dark as the high point of each day. Braving the haze of mosquitoes which hung over the valley, she would leave the ship and splash across to the far side of the stream. Always with the same purpose: to confront the dragonfly with its scarlet-tipped wings, which never failed to zoom down towards her and hover an arm's length from her face.

It was her favoured enemy, its many-lensed eyes telling her harsh truths about the forest and its inhabitants. Look at me, it seemed to say, and you will see your fate. And returning its fixed and knowing gaze, she came close to appreciating the human qualities of this creature – its controlled aggression, its fascination with the being it sought to destroy. Yes, I understand you, she wanted to say, except she lacked the necessary words. No words were needed to read the cruel intent in those eyes, however, each twilight encounter filling her with a secret thrill of dread; a thrill which, for a few fearful heartbeats, rescued her from that sea of uncaring that was sweeping her away.

Then, one evening – how long was it since Walter had gone? she had lost count of the weeks and days – the ritual of those twilight meetings suddenly changed. Instead of wading the stream and waiting for the dragonfly's arrival, she found it already there, hovering in its appointed place. At her approach it swung in closer than ever before. In order to threaten her? She couldn't decide; could no longer grasp the meaning in those eyes and in the altered angle of the body. All she knew for sure was that it was trying to tell her something. But what? That her time had finally come? That tonight would bring her long journey to a close?

The sun had not yet set, but a pale moon, wasted to a wafer thinness, had risen above the trees. On impulse she pointed towards it.

'See,' she said aloud. 'Nothing lasts. Not you, not me. Not anyone.'

Did the creature understand her? She only partly understood herself what it was she was saying. And in any case the dragonfly paid no attention. Its tufted wings merely whirred closer, until they were actually touching her, the blood-red tips fluttering softly against her cheek. Only for a few moments. Then, as always happened, it slipped away into the dusk.

She touched her cheek and looked at her fingers

in the failing light, half expecting to find them stained with blood. Was that the meaning of its touch? That the only bond which bound them now was a bloody one?

She thought so some minutes later, when the nightly chorus of the swarms shrilled through the darkening forest. For there was something different about it; the high whine no longer constant, but wavering slightly.

'What's going on?' Joe asked, detecting the difference in tone while they were securing the ship for the night.

'The patterns of sound have become more complex,' Trog replied.

'Yes, but what does that mean?' Joe insisted, turning to Anna.

She shrugged, remembering the touch of those blood-red wings. 'The worst, I expect,' she said, and went through to the other cabin, having already decided to spend this last night amongst the unborn.

They too, she suspected, had much to tell her if only she could learn to read their mute appeal; but like the dragonfly they dwelt in a realm beyond her reach, and all she could do was share their silence. Share with them and wait, burdened at this eleventh hour by regret that she had never felt the dabble of their fingers on her cheek, never once compared their soft touch with that of the dragonfly.

One mind, Walter had insisted in his talks with her, one voice. To which she was tempted to add, sadly, one touch. But before she could do so, Joe burst in upon her.

'There's something funny going on outside,' he whispered hoarsely. 'Listen!'

It was true. Walter had always referred to the

swarms' shrill cry as a song, but never before had it sounded so songlike, a hint of melody running through it.

'That isn't all,' Joe said. 'Come and take a look from in here.'

She followed him to the forward cabin where he shone a torch out into the night. The swarms had arrived en masse, insects in their teeming billions; but despite their increased numbers they were no longer pressing close around the hull. They had withdrawn slightly, their countless eyes glinting in the torchlight, as if they were more interested in observing the ship than entering it.

'What do you think?' Joe whispered. 'Is this the lull before the storm?'

She said nothing, detecting in those watchful eyes the same haunting expression she had seen in the eyes of the dragonfly.

Taking her silence for agreement, Joe put one arm around her shoulders. 'If the next few hours are as bad as I think they'll be,' he murmured, his voice unusually subdued, 'maybe now's the time to send our warning to Titan.'

On the point of agreeing, she stopped herself. 'No,' she said, though without quite understanding why. 'Not yet. Let's wait a while longer.'

'Wait?' he exclaimed miserably, and nearly lost control, the torch trembling in his hand. 'That's all we ever do! And where has it got us? We don't have much more time left, Anna. You must know that.'

Yes, she knew it, but still she restrained him when he tried to reach for the transmitter.

'Please,' she whispered, her lips close to his ear. 'Not yet. Not until we're sure.'

He clicked off the torch, and as the tension eased

from his body she drew him down beside her. Wide-eyed and wakeful, they clung wordlessly to each other in the dark. For one seemingly endless hour, and then another. Their vigil stretching on into the depths of the night, with nothing but the rise and fall of insect voices to mark the passage of time.

She didn't think it possible to fall asleep. She thought she had merely rested her head against Joe's shoulder. Yet when she looked up it was morning and they were lying crumpled together on the floor. Boots lay snuggled between them, and Trog was already busy in the tiny galley preparing breakfast.

It was the clatter he was making – the only sound throughout the ship – which brought home to her the peacefulness of the morning. As did the way Boots stretched lazily and stalked over to the door, ready to be let out.

She clambered hastily to her feet, disturbing Joe as she did so, and peered through the windscreen. The fresh new foliage on the far bank had been crushed to the ground, as if by a great weight of bodies, and several branches had been broken from nearby trees, but otherwise there was no sign of the insect armies that had swarmed around them during the night.

'They're gone!' she said, her tone a mixture of amazement and relief. 'They left without attacking!'

'Maybe they're just playing with us,' Joe suggested warily.

Yet somehow she knew that wasn't the answer.

'Come with me,' she said, and urged them all into the airlock.

It opened to a morning different from any she had ever experienced here in the forest. Although there was a stillness about this early hour, it was not the deathly stillness which usually descended upon the

235

valley at dawn. That deeper silence had vanished, as if spirited away in the night, and with it had gone the prevailing air of fear. Now, tiny fish flickered to and fro in the stream; birds called from high in the canopy; and for the first time in weeks the hooting cries of monkeys echoed amongst the trees.

'You don't think . . .?' Joe began, but she cut him short, sensing that it was too soon to jump to conclusions.

'Scan the other ships for us, Trog,' she said. 'Tell us what you find.'

His head tilted towards the hillside and rotated rapidly.

'No life-forms detectable in any of the ships,' he reported.

'None? You're certain of that?'

'Impossible to be certain. I can report only a high probability factor.'

'Well, let's test it,' Anna said, and marched resolutely up the hill to the nearest hulk.

She entered with some nervousness, but as Trog had predicted it was empty. The slightly acrid scent of insect bodies was all that remained.

It was the same in the other ships, their dark interiors occupied only by tumbled equipment and boxes of supplies.

'They're gone,' Joe said wonderingly as they emerged from the last of the hulks. 'There isn't an insect left here.'

'Incorrect,' Trog pointed out. 'The swarms have dispersed, that is all. Normal insect activity continues in soil and plants.'

'Normal? What's that supposed to mean?'

'Ecosystem cannot function without input from insects,' Trog explained.

'Let's see how far this normal activity extends,' Anna said, and set out along the valley, following the meandering line of the stream.

For half an hour they walked in silence, with Trog scanning their surroundings every few minutes, and still there was no sign of the swarms. As Trog had predicted earlier, they had dispersed, their countless numbers merging into the larger existence of the forest. And with that merging process had come a change, that portion of the forest stirring into life, rapidly shaking off the fears of the past and revealing its hidden riches for the first time in centuries.

Never was that more evident than when Anna and Joe spied the big cat. Returning along a sandy section of the stream, they heard a crackle of leaves from somewhere up ahead, and a sleek shape slid out from amongst the trees.

'There!' Anna hissed, and pointed to where the cat, its shoulders hunched, was crouched at the water's edge, drinking.

It looked up at the sound of her voice, gazing at them with untroubled eyes before stooping again to the stream. Only when its thirst was satisfied did it turn and pick its way slowly back into the forest.

'I've never seen that happen before,' Joe breathed. 'The way it just walked out into the open! It wasn't scared at all. And did you notice how it took its time? Surely that has to mean . . .'

But again she cut him short, not yet daring to hope.

'We'll see,' she said vaguely.

She intended waiting at least another night or two before making up her mind, but as they neared the ship something happened which eclipsed all her doubts. There was a twinkle of rainbowed light, a flash of scarlet, and a dragonfly appeared out of nowhere. It hovered for a fraction of a second; then, with a quick decisive movement, it landed on her wrist, its touch so delicate, so weightless, that she felt almost buoyed up by it. Again it had no words for her, but now she needed none. She had finally understood its message. In sitting there on her bare skin, happy in her presence, it was treating her as it would a plant or tree or any member of its own kind. And in that instant she knew that Walter had been successful. Against all the odds he had reached the Palaces, spoken to the Queens, and explained the strange kinship that now reigned throughout the planet.

Turning her head slowly so as not to scare the dragonfly, she said in a low voice: 'Go and activate the incubators, Trog. It's time.'

Then to Joe, who continued to stare at her wrist with startled eyes: 'I think we should send our message to Titan now.'

He wrenched his eyes from the quivering wings, the beginnings of a smile on his face. 'What should we say?'

'Tell them . . .' she began, and hesitated, struggling to recall something Walter had said once. Ah yes, that was it, so simple really. 'Just say that all is well.'

★   ★   ★

Two children were born the day Walter and Og returned. Anna and Joe were sitting quietly beside the ship, the babies cradled in their arms, when the familiar voices floated along the valley towards them.

'Listen,' Anna said, for even at a distance she had recognised the melody. It was the same weird song

238

that the swarms had sung on the night before they dispersed.

'Why that song?' Joe asked as they set out along the stream together.

'I expect it's Walter's way of saying we're all one and the same,' Anna answered with a smile. 'You must remember how he was always going on about one mind.'

'How can I ever forget?' Joe said, and laughed.

As they rounded the nearest bend they caught their first glimpse of him. Trundling along the bed of the stream about a hundred metres away, he looked more dilapidated than ever. His windscreen was smashed, his sides dented and streaked with rust, and one of his engines must have failed and been discarded, because now he was partly supported by Og who tramped along with the prow resting across his shoulders. Og, too, was not in good condition. His left arm hung slackly at his side and his right leg dragged a little at every step.

Yet it was none of these details which made Anna and Joe gaze in wonderment at the approaching craft. It was the butterflies. Tens of thousands of them. Fluttering and dancing in the sunlight, they played endlessly about Walter's battered hull, their multi-coloured wings giving to his rust-streaked plates a touch of splendour.

About the author

With a host of award-winning novels to his credit,
Victor Kelleher remains one of Australia's most cel-
ebrated writers for both adults and children. Born in
London, he lived in Africa for twenty years before
moving to New Zealand where he began to write,
prompted by homesickness for Africa. He moved to
Australia in 1976.

Victor's first book for young people was *Forbidden
Paths of Thual* and since then his novels have received
many awards and commendations. His prizes have
included the Australian Children's Book of the Year
Award and the Australian Science Fiction Achieve-
ment Award. More recently, *Parkland* was shortlisted
for the 1995 Australian Children's Book of the Year
Award. Formerly an associate professor, he now
writes full time.